# NANNY & THE BEAST

## A BILLIONAIRE MAFIA ROMANCE

GEORGIA LE CARRE

Nanny & The Beast



978-1-910575-83-3

*For*

*Elizabeth Burns*

*He is only in the next room, babe.*

*You'll meet again.*

## ALSO BY GEORGIA

**The Billionaire Banker Series**

Owned

42 Days

Besotted

Seduce Me

Love's Sacrifice

Masquerade

**Pretty Wicked (novella)**

**Disfigured Love**

**Hypnotized**

**Crystal Jake 1,2&3**

**Sexy Beast**

**Wounded Beast**

**Beautiful Beast**

**Dirty Aristocrat**

**You Don't Own Me 1 & 2**

**You Don't Know Me**

**Blind Reader Wanted**

**The Bad Boy Wants Me**

**Submitting To The Billionaire**
**Redemption**
**The Heir**
**Blackmailed By The Beast**
**His Frozen Heart**

# CHAPTER 1

## APRIL

The address was only a short walk from the Knightsbridge tube station. The sun was shining as I took the little path that led to the private square called Little Sion. In no time, I was standing in front of a large set of wrought iron electric gates adorned on either side by stone lions set on tall pillars. Before I could press the intercom button, a voice with a foreign accent brusquely instructed me to go through the small side gate.

Okay.

As I got to the gate, it clicked open. I pushed it, and walked through. Standing on the asphalt driveway for a second, I looked up at the mansion. Wow! Painted brilliant white, it practically glinted in the sun. As if it were some ice palace from a fairy tale. Who'd have thought such a massive palace existed right in the heart of Knightsbridge.

A huge bald man wearing an earpiece and a black suit that was a size too small for him was making his way towards me. The guy was so big the top of my head only came up to his tree-trunk biceps. Of course, as basic human interaction demanded, I smiled politely at him.

He didn't smile back as he let his eyes dart over me suspiciously.

Okay. Be like that then. "I've come about the job. I have an appointment with Mr. Volkov," I said.

He grunted. "I know. Come with me." He turned on his heel.

I fell into step beside him. Actually, it was more like a jog, or to be even more accurate, a fast-paced sprint. Damn him. "My name is April Winters, what's yours?" I gasped, in an effort to be civil and pretend the speed we were travelling at was my normal pace.

He grunted again, before his eyes slid down to me. The expression on his face didn't change. "Brain," he said.

I mean, I could have said, 'what', or laughed outright, or if I wanted to carry on being polite and civil, 'pardon me', but I kinda knew I'd heard right. Somehow, the name suited him to a T. Of course, he would be called Brain.

I gave up any pretense of civility at that point, and silently followed him up to the house.

Two more 'brains' in black suits watched us from the entrance of the house. They wore the same expressions of extreme distrust.

For the first time, I wondered what the hell I had got myself into.

Who was my employer?

Obviously, the first thing I did when I was told I'd been

selected to apply for this job was Google Yuri Volkov. All I found were images of an extraordinarily handsome businessman escorting beautiful women to high society parties. No mention of a palace in Knightsbridge, or goons that behaved as if they belonged in a bad Mafia movie.

Come to think of it now, in every photo I did come across he was unsmiling, giving me the impression of a cold, aloof man. Still not every rich, unsmiling Russian is a mobster or a money launderer. None of that bothered me any.

If I got the job, I would be in charge of his niece and report her progress to him. And that was all I would be doing. Since I was extremely good at my job, I didn't foresee needing to take shit from Mr. Volkov.

There was one picture of him though, playing polo in Windsor, which caught my attention. Something about the expression in his eyes as he leaned down to swing his mallet. Here was a man who got what he wanted. An implacable man. A man you did not antagonize.

A man you allowed into your body.

Did I just go there?

I crushed the thought.

I was a professional, and I had no intention of ever being anything else. Under no circumstances was I exchanging my good reputation for any man. No matter how hot he was. Besides, it wasn't as if a man like that would ever give a woman like me a second look. All those beautiful women swarming around him like flies to shit. Not a chance.

Which obviously was a good thing.

The last thing I needed was temptation.

Not that I'm saying I was tempted.

The man opened the grand doors and my jaw dropped. Jesus! Mr. Volkov must be a very, very successful businessman. If the exterior was impressive, the interior of his abode made me feel like I had just stepped into an episode of The Secret Lives of Billionaires. It had one of those foyers with a wide spiral staircase. From the glass ceiling four floors up, hung the biggest chandelier I'd ever seen in my life. It seemed to have millions of crystal pieces that caught the sunlight streaming in from the top and practically blazed like it was on fire.

Our shoes rang on the marble floors. Some poor minion had polished them so hard I was afraid Brain would be able to see up my skirt. Fortunately, he kept his eyes ahead. We turned into a room, which I suppose could be called a music room, since there was a gleaming grand piano in it.

"Wait here until you are called," Brain said.

There were two women sitting on the fine chairs in the room. I recognized one of them. Mary Sedgewick from Caring Nannies. She was generally accepted as their best asset. She looked at me with a smug expression. The other woman, I didn't know, but I guessed she must be from Sarah Bright's agency, because she was holding a file with their logo on it. She nodded at me formally.

I smiled at them both and took a seat on one of the armchairs. It was upholstered in sunshine yellow and was incredibly comfortable. Funny thing. I suddenly felt nervous. I took a mint out of my handbag and popped it into my mouth.

A middle-aged woman in a severe navy-blue suit came into the room. "Ms. Sedgewick, please come with me."

Mary stood and with a confident smile walked up to her.

The door closed behind them, and I turned my attention to the French windows. Outside, stone steps led to a formal garden that seemed to stretch endlessly. There was a fountain. I stared at it blankly. Ten minutes later, the woman in the navy-blue suit was back, which surprised me. Maybe Mary didn't get the job, after all.

"Miss Winters," she said with a smile.

I smiled back, stood up, smoothed my skirt over my thighs, and walked towards her. She introduced herself as, Mrs. Misha Gorev. She was one of Mr. Volkov's personal assistants.

If this job wasn't Mary's, I felt confident it would be mine.

I was good at my job. They called me the child whisperer back at the agency. I had tamed spoilt, rich kids, brats with behavioral problems, sick kids. So far, no kid had defeated me. I straightened my back as Mrs. Gorev's hand closed over the intricately carved, gold door handle. The door opened and the wind left my lungs.

Good Lord! It must be the devil himself sitting behind the desk, because only the devil could be so darkly handsome.

# CHAPTER 2

## YURI

https://www.youtube.com/watch?v=SGyOaCXr8Lw
(You Make A Grown Man Cry)

As the door opened further, I looked up from the file in front of me. Beyond Misha was the next candidate. My eyes found hers and for a second my brain stopped functioning. Three things:

First: she looked *nothing* like the photograph in her file.

Second: she wasn't one of the classical beauties I usually hooked up with.

Third: lust. Pure, unadulterated lust flowed like fire in my veins.

God, I wanted this woman!

She smiled and it might just be the sexiest thing a woman had ever done with her lips. Actually, she looked like she belonged in a Raphael painting. Huge green eyes, flaming red hair, and skin like thick cream.

My gaze ran down her body. Even in the cheap shirt buttoned up to her neck and loose gray suit she was sexy as fuck. I leaned in my chair making it tip back. "Come in and take a seat, Miss Winters."

She walked with a sure feline glide, towards one of the two chairs in front of my desk and sank into it. "Thank you." Her voice was soft and mysterious.

"So, tell me about yourself?" I invited, trying to keep my eyes from wandering.

"Well, there's not that much to tell. I am a teacher by profession, but I decided that I preferred working with small children, so I became a nanny."

"Why?"

Her enormous eyes regarded me steadily. "What do you mean?"

"Why do you prefer working with small children?"

She shrugged. "I don't know. Nobody has really asked me that. I think it's because I love their innocence. I find them honest and easy to deal with."

"You don't like dealing with adults?"

She shifted in her chair. "Not so much."

"Why not?"

"Like I said. I find people often have hidden motives, and they're not very honest most of the time."

"So you like honesty."

Her gaze was direct and sincere. "Always."

"That will be all, Miss Winters." I stood. "Thank you for your time."

She didn't stand from her chair. "That's it?"

"Yes, Misha will contact you on Monday and let you know the outcome of the interview."

Her eyes widened.

God, they were fucking beautiful. I felt my cock twitch and come alive. I definitely made the right decision. She was far too distracting to be working in this house. I don't need that kind of temptation.

She stood suddenly, her eyes flashing. "Why do I need to wait for Mrs. Gorev to let me know? Be honest. Just tell me I didn't get the job. That way, I won't have to stress about it over the weekend."

I nod. "Very well. You didn't get the job."

"Why?" she demanded.

I couldn't remember the last time anybody questioned me this aggressively. I wasn't sure how I felt about it, it niggled at my sense of absolute authority and control, but I did feel intrigued. Very intrigued. "Do you want me to be honest, Miss Winters?"

"Naturally."

I walked around the desk, and she took a step back. The move was instinctive and told me clearly, the lust I felt wasn't one-sided. She wanted me too. We faced each other, and I felt it instantly. We were natural born adversaries. We'd fight like cats and dogs at every turn. Even if I wanted to hire her, I couldn't.

"Because …" I said, and shot out a hand. My movement so quick and unexpected, she didn't even have a chance to react. I pulled her towards me and her luscious curves slammed into my body. So hard, she gasped, her mouth falling open with astonishment…and excitement. No mistaking that!

"Of this," I murmured as my mouth crashed down on hers.

For at least a whole instant, she remained so shocked she was frozen, then she began to struggle.

I didn't let go. I waited for the natural desire between us to burst into flames.

And it did.

Unfortunately, it wasn't what I thought it would be.

It wasn't a fire, it was a volcano that erupted between our bodies. We devoured each other, my hands slipped to her ass and squeezed. It was a fine ass. I could already see it bare and my palm-print on it. I could tell she was completely and utterly lost. I could have taken her right there on my desk.

And I would have.

If I didn't have the urgent problem of finding a nanny for little Yulia. No, I'll save this flower for later. I lifted my head and looked into her eyes. They were half-dazed with lust. Yes, she was irretrievably lost.

She blinked. Once, twice, thrice.

Then she made her own move. She stepped back, swung her arm forward, and caught my cheek in a stinging slap.

It would've galled her to know, I could have stopped her hand at any time from the moment she decided to do it, but I wanted to feel the violence I had aroused in her. It felt good to see her face become pale when she realized what she'd done. No one had ever caused her to lose control in that way before. The kiss was one thing. The slap. She'd never imagined herself capable of such a base thing as violence. A pulse fluttered like a bird in her throat.

I smiled.

She stared at me in disbelief for another few seconds, then she turned on her heel and walked quickly out. She didn't bother to close the door so I watched her ramrod straight back as she crossed the music room. As she got halfway down the room, I saw a small figure slip out from behind the heavy curtains and approach her.

The affronted nanny came to a sudden stop.

As I watched in amazement, my niece curled her hand around April Winter's middle finger and looked up at her.

Oh, fuck!

## CHAPTER 3

## APRIL

Blood was rushing so fast in my veins I could feel it thundering in my ears as I stared down in amazement at the little child staring up at me. I knew immediately who she was. She was the niece, the girl I was supposed to care for. Her eyes were dark pools of some deep emotion, and yet she took the bold step of slipping her cold little hand into mine.

In an instant, I forgot what had happened a few moments ago. Poor little thing was suffering. I took a deep breath. No matter how I felt about her uncle, I had to be as gentle with her as I would have been with a spooked deer. "Hello."

From a pocket in her dress, she fished out a small pad. It had a pencil hanging off it by a ribbon and began to write on it. Solemnly, she tore off the page and handed it to me.

Don't Go

I shook my head and looked at her sadly. Something about her tugged at my heart. It made me hate her uncle even more. "I'm sorry, but I have to go."

Her chin wobbled and her eyes filled with tears. She sniffed and wrote even more furiously on her pad. Tearing it off, she held it out to me.

I took it and read it.

Don't leave me

I got down on my haunches. "It's not that I want to leave you, but I didn't get the—"

"Miss Winters," a deep voice called from behind me.

The child jumped, then gave me one last imploring look before she ran away.

I straightened. I could feel my anger return as quickly as it had gone when the child approached me. I turned around.

Yuri Volkov's tall, intimidating frame was filling the doorway to his office. There was no expression on his handsome face. "Will you come into my study, please?"

I didn't want to go. I honestly didn't, but I felt my feet move as if I was a puppet on a string. I had no control. As I reached the door to his dark-wood paneled study, he took a step back to allow me to enter.

I passed him by and felt something. Like a crackle of electricity. It went right through my body. Doing my best to remain calm and composed, I turned around and faced him. I felt he could see right through me, even though I knew better.

"May I see the notes my niece gave you?"

He both intimidated and enticed me. Silently, I held out the crumpled papers in my palm.

He took them without letting our skin touch and glanced at them. His other hand came up to stroke his chin.

I stared at him.

When he looked up, his sensuous lips quirked upwards. Yuri Volkov smiling was another matter altogether. He was beautiful in the way a growling panther was. "I've reconsidered. I might have been too hasty in dismissing your services." His voice was so smooth and controlled no one would have believed that only minutes ago his tongue was in my mouth and I was mindlessly sucking on it.

"I'm afraid so have I," I said, relishing the new and heady power I held in my hands.

A flicker of annoyance crossed his expression. Something he put away very swiftly. It was clear he didn't have to deal with insubordination too often. As a matter of fact, he probably never had to deal with it.

"I'll double your salary."

"Thanks, but I think I'll pass."

"Name your own price then."

I wanted to remain impervious to all his offers, but my eyebrows shot upwards. "Are you serious?"

"Of course."

I didn't have to think about it. "No. You know it's not the money," I bit out.

"Then what would cause you to deny a child in need?"

"It's you," I said simply. "I couldn't possibly work for a man like you."

"Why not? You were perfectly willing a few minutes ago."

"That was before you forced yourself on me."

"I kissed you because *you* forced the issue. You wanted to know why I didn't want to hire you so I showed you why," he defended calmly.

"Well then, surely nothing has changed from a few minutes ago."

"A lot has changed. I take my responsibility for my niece very seriously. Nothing is more important. Yulia's needs have to be placed before mine at all times. Yes, I am sexually attracted to you, but I can get a woman from anywhere. She chose you, so her need to have you overrides mine."

For some strange reason the statement of how he could get a woman from anywhere cut me.

"As you are already aware from the job description," he continued, "my niece hasn't spoken a word for six months. No one, not even her psychiatrist knows why she won't talk. Neither has she made any attempt to befriend anyone. You're the first person she appears to have connected with and show a need for, so I will move heaven and earth to see that she gets what she wants. I believe you might hold the key to her coming out of her shell and talking again."

I could tell he was telling the truth and I believed him when he said he was putting her needs before his. I even felt a touch of admiration and yet…I stared at him.

I felt torn. On one hand, I wanted to stay. I could still see the fear in his niece's eyes. It'd taken a lot for her to approach me and yet she had. It seemed important to her to make me stay. Why me I didn't know. But I wanted to get to the mystery of why she had chosen me. I wanted to help too. It was what had drawn me to this job in the first place.

On the other hand, some instinct for self-preservation told me to get the hell out of here. This man could be very dangerous to my sanity. Within minutes of being in his presence he'd made me lose control and behave in a fashion, I had never before even imagined acting. I never dreamed I could be provoked to hurt another human being.

"You can be certain if you take the job you will have no unwanted advances from me," he added, as if he could read my mind.

I bit my lip uncertainly.

"Please, Miss Winters," he said softly, persuasively.

I could see how fiercely intense his desire for me to stay and help his niece was.

To hear this powerful man plead was something else. I realized he must really love his niece. "Do you promise that you will never again pull another stunt like that?"

"You have my word."

I nodded slowly. "All right, Mr. Volkov. I'll stay and see how it goes, but if you ever—"

"I gave you my word. If anything happens between us, it will be because you initiated it."

"It will be a cold day in hell before that happens."

"Then you have nothing to worry about. Will you be able to start tomorrow?"

"I guess so."

"I will send a car around to pick you up."

"No, don't do that I'll get here on my own."

"As you wish. My secretary will take it from here and get you to sign the necessary paperwork."

"Fine."

"Thank you, Miss Winters." He nodded formally, distantly, then went to open the door for me.

I was frozen to the spot.

"Until tomorrow, Miss Winters." He looked at me with the politeness of a stranger. It was as if a door had closed and a part of me grieved. Before this agreement, he was a man and I was a woman, now he was my employer and I was his employee.

I walked away from him and I couldn't shake the feeling I had lost something important. I told myself I was being silly. I should be happy. I got the job I wanted, but inside me there was an ache, a longing for something I, myself had thrown away too hastily.

# CHAPTER 4

## APRIL

"He did what?" Charlotte, my roommate, popped her head out from the bathroom door, a green sheet mask on her face.

Charlotte and I were school friends who became teachers, didn't really like it, and waded into the nanny business together. Between us, we'd changed a truckload of diapers, been peed on by countless infants, had innumerable encounters with smirking, badly behaved toddlers; and dealt with a few jealous wives and their overly-friendly husbands into the bargain.

In temperament though, we are chalk and cheese. I'm a calm, cautious, thoughtful redhead, and she's a risk taking, energetic, fiery blonde. Her temper is legendary. Back at school, she used to terrify even the boys, but what they didn't know was underneath it all, she had a heart of gold. She is the most loyal, kind, and supportive friend one could ever hope to have.

"You heard me," I said, kicking off my sensible pumps and heading for the fridge.

"No I couldn't have, because I thought I heard you say Yuri Volkov *kissed* you."

I opened the fridge and turned to look at her. "Yeah, that's what I said."

Her mouth opened in astonishment, and the mask started to slip.

The sight registered as comical even on my tightly strung nerves. I had to laugh.

"Why *exactly* are you laughing?" she demanded.

I grabbed two bottles of beer. "That mask! You look creepy...and a bit insane!"

"Oh," she acknowledged. Realigning the cutouts to fit over her eyes, nose and lips, she came over to the living room, took the beer I held out, and plopped unto the couch beside me. "Let me get this straight… you went for an interview to be his niece's nanny and he *kissed* you*!*"

"Uh, huh."

Charlotte toasted me with her bottle. "What do you mean by kissed? On the cheek like the French and Italians, on the forehead like fussy grandmothers, or…"

"On the mouth," I finished.

"Whoa!"

I took a sip of cold beer and savored the sensation of it sliding down my parched throat.

"Okay, so tell me exactly what happened." She grabbed a half-eaten container of Pringles off the coffee table and popped one into her mouth.

With my eyes to the ceiling, I began, "It was a hot summer's day—"

She threw a Pringle at me. "Stop deflecting!"

I fished the fluffy chip off the couch and munched it absently. "To be honest, it's all kind of blurry right now. One minute we were talking in his expensive study and the next he'd come around and—"

"Oh my God," she spat. "What a bastard. You should report him to the police. That's sexual harassment right there."

"It wasn't as bad as that, Charlotte."

She waited for me to explain, but when I didn't, she frowned. "What do you mean it wasn't as bad as that? You don't think it's harassment when a complete stranger who is supposed to be interviewing you for a job to take care of his niece, jumps on you like that?"

"I'm not sure what I think exactly."

At her dumbstruck gaze, a mad giggle escaped my lips. I was probably still in shock. Nothing I'd learned and known about myself in my twenty-six years had prepared me for the way my body reacted to Yuri Volkov. For heaven's sake, I didn't even like the man. Yes, he was physically beautiful, but he was too hard and cold. I liked my men warm and caring. This was my first experience with pure lust.

She put the tub of Pringles down and folded her arms across her chest. "I have ten more minutes before I have to take off this mask. You better make me understand what happened, or I'm doing everything I can to get him thrown in jail, and you perhaps…into a psychiatric ward."

"What did I do?" I cried, trying not to laugh at how angry she was becoming on my behalf.

She glared at me. "You can laugh and pretend all you want, but your eyes give it away. You look haunted, young lady. I'm not playing this game. What did that monster do to you? Spit it out."

"Okay, okay. Calm down. First of all, he's not a monster. It wasn't like that."

"Then tell me how it was before I explode."

"Okay, I arrived at his house. Actually, calling it a house is like calling Kim Kardashian a housewife. It was a very grand, nouveau riche mansion. It even had a massive bodyguard called Brain—"

"Are you trying to be funny?" Charlotte interrupted, rising angrily from her seat.

Charlotte's rage made me feel bad. She couldn't help it. She flew into a temper if she thought anybody was trying to take advantage of me. In remorse, I pulled her back down. "Relax, will you? There really was a bodyguard called Brain, and I *am* getting to the important bits. It's just that my brain is a bit fried so it helps to try and recall the details—"

"Why is your brain fried?"

"Yuri Volkov *kissed* me," I reminded her flatly.

Her eyes narrowed to slits, a feat considering how enormous

her eyes were. “I thought you weren’t feeling harassed about it.”

“It depends—”

“On what?” she flared up again, hands on hips.

“On your definition of harassed. Anyway, can I just get through my story without being constantly interrupted?” I glanced at my watch. “I believe I have seven minutes left.”

“Fine. Carry on.” She reached for her Pringles.

“Where was I?”

“A bodyguard called Brain. I assume he was as thick as two short planks,” she said sarcastically.

I grinned. “He did give the impression intellectual pursuits were not his thing.”

She smiled, relaxing a little. “Before you carry on, did you meet the child?”

I nodded and frowned, remembering Yulia’s silent, but desperate plea.

“Did you find out why she won’t speak?”

I shook my head. “No. Apparently, no one knows, not even her psychiatrist. She seems to communicate by writing on her notepad.”

For a second, my train of thought returned to the ivory marble room with its intricate Persian carpets, golden side tables, and gigantic vases of exotic flowers. In all my life, I’d never felt my heart beat so frantically as I strode through it. And then that moment when I went from shock, sexual arousal, horror, and confusion to looking into the deeply troubled eyes of a sad, little Princess. She didn't smile. She didn't speak. She didn't need to. Her eyes said it all.

Charlotte took an agonized breath and nudged, "Earth to April..."

I lifted my gaze to hers. "Sorry. Her name is Yulia. It was the weirdest thing but she ran up to me after I left Mr. Volkov's study and put her hand in mine. Then she wrote on her pad, *Don't go* and gave it to me."

Charlotte's eyes were as wide as I'd ever seen them. "Good heavens, that's like something from a Disney movie. What did you freaking do?"

I took a sip of beer as I thought about the strange, surreal moment. "Nothing at first. I was too stunned. I didn't think I could work for her uncle. Not after I slapped him."

Charlotte clapped her hand on her mouth. "You slapped him. Okay, back up, back up. Let's go back to the uncle and the kiss."

# CHAPTER 5

## APRIL

Charlotte gulped down her beer and watched me with unblinking attention while I told her about the shortest, strangest interview I've had with the most mysterious man I'd ever met.

"He sounds creepy," she decided.

"Trust me, creepy is the last word anyone would use to describe him."

"What word would you use?"

"I don't know if I can describe him with one word. To start with, he was extremely difficult to read. Like trying to suss out the Mona Lisa or the Sphinx." I shook my head. "No, that's not quite right either. The whole episode was almost like a scene from *The Interview With A Vampire*. The whole time there was an underlying dark sexual tension."

Charlotte leaned forward. "Really?"

"Well, for all the five minutes I was there anyway. Then he informed me the interview was over and his PA would contact me with me the result." I crinkled my face. "Basically, don't call us, we'll call you."

"Why? He didn't even give you a chance."

"That's exactly what I thought and it made me so angry at the arrogance with which he was dismissing me that I forced him to confirm I didn't have the job."

Charlotte's eyes widened as she slipped a Pringle into her mouth. "Go you! *Then* what happened?"

"The next thing I knew he'd left his seat, come around to my side, and grabbed me. He has very strong arms, like steel bands."

"I'm sure he has," she murmured staring at me.

"Before I even knew what was happening I heard him say, 'because of this.' Then his mouth swooped down on mine. I was too shocked to do anything about it."

As I spoke, I remembered the burn of his cold eyes, and the fiery sizzle of arousal in the air. I felt his sensuous mouth on mine, the hardness of body pressed against mine, and the vortex of desire that I fell into. Clearly, I recalled the glint of triumph in his eyes as my hand connected with his cheek. As if he'd wanted me to slap him. Which of course, was madness.

"You're kidding?" Charlotte breathed.

"I'm not."

"That's so…out there, but hold that thought for a moment," she said, jumping up. "I need another beer. I'll be back." Charlotte scooted into the kitchen and returned with two beers, one of which she slapped into my hand. She dropped into her chair and pulled her feet under her. "Proceed," she invited. "You were telling me how Yuri kissed you. This is the good part, so don't hold back. I want all the details. As many as you can spare."

I stared at her eager face and realized I couldn't share that moment with her. She already thought he was a creep and my reaction as deserving a place in a psychiatric ward. How could I make her understand I had absolutely no control over my own actions? That a complete stranger could have had me right there on the floor of his study. I didn't even have the excuse of being drunk. I felt myself blush with shame. "There is not much to tell. It was just wrong."

Charlotte's eyes turned penetrating. I never could hide anything from her. "Just wrong? That's it. You didn't feel anything? Every kiss does something. You can kiss a frog and still get something."

"Well, he got slapped."

"Hmmm...yes. You said. So that's it then. You didn't get the job."

"No, I got the job."

She looked incredulous. "He gave you the job after you slapped him?"

"Well, after I slapped him I left his office, but that was when I met his niece. She ran up to me and gave me the notes. Of course, he saw our exchange and called me back into his office. He said he had reconsidered and was going to give me the job because he wanted to put Yulia's needs above his."

"How magnanimous of him," Charlotte replied sarcastically.

"And you're okay with this?" She seemed to be waiting with bated breath.

I sighed. "Yes."

"Why? He sounds extremely misogynistic and manipulative."

"I don't know how to put this, but I'm actually quite concerned about a little girl who won't talk. A little girl who thinks I, a complete stranger, might be the answer to her prayers. I'm also very curious to know why she chose me. Maybe I was simply a face she preferred to the other applicants, or there's a mystery I can help to solve. In any case, she moved me."

Charlotte bit her lip. "I still don't know how I feel about the lecherous uncle, but I think the child made a brilliant decision picking you. You will be good for her."

"You really think so?"

"Absolutely. They don't call you the child whisperer at the agency for nothing. You'll help her. I'm sure of it."

We were silent for a few seconds.

"What does he look like in real life… the uncle?" she asked softly.

My breath came out in a rush. "Sexy. Dark hair. Blue eyes, cold and piercing. Full lips, chiseled jawline, clean shaven, straight nose, and his eyes are so blue, cold and piercing..."

"You mentioned that." Charlotte giggled.

"Really tall too... six feet three or maybe even more. I only came up to his chest."

"Dangerous looking?"

"Extremely. I was quaking when he came close to me." I shifted uncomfortably. Even since that kiss, my clit felt strangely swollen. Now even the mere thought of him was making it throb.

"So you really wanted him, huh?" Charlotte deduced, her eyes astonished and baffled. As if she was finding out, I wasn't the person she'd spent her whole life believing I was.

I gazed into her dear and familiar eyes. Those kind eyes I always knew I could trust with my life, and suddenly I was ashamed for entertaining the thought of not being honest with her. It was Yuri Volkov's fault. Never before had a man come between us. No, I didn't want to hide how I really felt about him from her. Charlotte wasn't just my best friend and roommate; she was the sister I never had.

"I wasn't very honest just now when I said I felt nothing when he kissed me. The truth is I don't think I've ever felt that much attraction to someone in my entire life," I confessed.

"Wow, I've never seen you like this," she said thoughtfully.

"I've never felt like this before. Oh Charlotte, I wanted to *fuck* him right there."

Charlotte's hand flew to her mouth. "Oh, my God!"

"There were goosebumps down my neck and arms," I continued. "I didn't think he would notice, but his eyes traced them... He knew. It was so crazy. I could smell his need—"

Charlotte's giggle brought me back to the room. "You could smell his need? What are you? A she-wolf?"

I smiled weakly. "I swear I could...it's hard to explain."

"I know. You had to be there."

"Yes, I felt like I was on fire. I don't know how it happened, but when his lips met mine, I felt as if I was melting. I couldn't even feel my legs. There was literally fire in the pit of my stomach... I really thought I was going to pass out. All I wanted to do was have him inside me. Just once... not more. He'll ruin me, otherwise."

"And I want to watch," the words slipped out before she realized it. Our eyes clashed before she could regain her senses.

I shot out my feet and kicked her off the couch. "Get out, you creep. Your ten minutes are over."

Laughing, she pulled the mask off her face and hurried away from my attack. "I'm not even going to take that back. From all you've said, assuming you weren't exaggerating, I'd pay money to watch him pounding into you... you grabbing those thick muscles for dear life..."

"Get out!" I yelled, throwing a cushion at her.

She dodged it and went on teasing me. "The tight walls of your pussy milking his hard, thick cock."

"You're sick."

"Oh, wait—" She stopped suddenly and looked very worried. "What if he has a small cock?"

"Get lost," I added, throwing another cushion at her.

She laughingly evaded it. "Now that would make an excellent end to this story."

"It's already ended. We agreed that he would not pursue me. He gave me his word. And I believed him."

"No, no, no," she cried dramatically. "We need an ending to this story. Is his cock big or not?"

"I'm going there to be the nanny of a seriously unhappy little girl, not report to you on the size of his cock."

Her smile was demonic. "You've obviously never heard of multi-tasking."

"Never heard the word," I denied, amused in spite of myself.

She sobered up. "On a serious note, you do realize I was only fooling around. I don't expect you to sleep with your boss. In fact, while you were at your interview I did a little research and—"

"In the tabloids? Are you kidding me?"

"They're not entirely wrong about everything," she defended. "And the word is Yuri Volkov is somehow connected to the Russian Mafia."

"I did my research too and I never found any mention of that. Are these the same tabloids that claim the Queen is a reptilian?"

"First of all, you were probably distracted by his looks and stopped your investigation there. Secondly, I got the reptilian stuff from the History channel, actually if you look closely at the Queen—"

I laughed and started walking out of the room. "Enough, enough! I have to pack."

Charlotte followed me. "You know the Mafia don't take prisoners. They kill their victims!"

For a second, I thought about the dark amusement on Yuri

Volkov's face as I stood in front of him shaking with horror at my own violence. Then I put it away and turned around. "You really have to stop reading the tabloids."

"I told you I didn't get that from the tabloids. I watched all The Godfather movies."

I sighed heavily.

"I'm serious, April. I know I was clowning around just now about his cock, but I didn't mean any of it. Sleeping with your boss is a very, very bad idea. You will keep your wits about you, won't you?"

I smiled gently. "I will and thank you for caring about me."

She didn't smile back. "You're sure you trust this man's word?"

"Have you ever met a man that made you feel safe? As if no one would dare lay a finger on you because you were with him."

She shook her head silently.

"Want to know something weird?"

She nodded slowly.

"While I was with Yuri, he made me feel safe, absolutely, and completely safe. For that moment, I was his woman and every other man knew not to even come near his possession."

"I wasn't worrying about other people laying a finger on you. I was worrying about him and what he could do to you," she stated solemnly.

# CHAPTER 6

## APRIL

The sun was bright and the sky clear blue, dotted with fluffy clouds when I arrived at the tall black gates of Yuri's mansion. I stood and stared at the steel spikes topping the high brick wall. I wouldn't be surprised at all, if there was electricity racing atop the wall. Certainly, they looked sharp enough to skewer any thief stupid enough to try climbing it.

Without me walking over to the intercom and identifying myself, the big gates swung open to admit me. Pulling my suitcase along, I strolled past the cultured garden towards the huge double doors.

There seemed to be no one around, or any visible surveillance cameras and it gave the impression the compound was without security, but I believed my every step was watched. A quick dart of my head in certain directions twice revealed the tail end of a dark suit, and a glistening pair of black shoes. There was intense security. *Everywhere.* They'd just been trained to ensure visitors didn't notice them.

It made me grow strangely wary of the man who'd made me catch fire yesterday. Yesterday seemed a lifetime ago. I had viewed the job like a ripe plum. It intrigued me. Would I be able to make the little girl talk again? I came here full of confidence and professionalism.

And I'd lost it all in his study.

Charlotte's warning rang in my ear. Somehow, the danger seemed even more real today. Before it'd been dimmed by my sole focus on the interview and its outcome. I took a deep breath and tightened my hold on the handle of my suitcase.

This would just be my residence for a bit and for a bit, its owner would be my master, perhaps even in more ways than I currently wanted to consider. I didn't allow myself to think further about it, but it was always there at the back of my mind. Subtle, but growing.

If things got complicated, I could always leave. I was free to walk away any time I wanted, but a voice in my head taunted. Are you really? It's true. I already felt more like a prisoner to Yuri's lust than his employee.

Brain came from the side of the house and walked up to me. There was no smile on his face. His thick muscles bulged against his badly cut suit. He looked more thug like than ever. He limited his greeting to a simple phrase, "Got any more bags?"

"No."

He reached for my bag and I let him have it.

He didn't wheel it, but carried it as if it weighed nothing. It looked very small compared to his great bulk. He unlocked the front door using a keypad.

"Can I get the code?" I asked.

"I have no instructions about that," he answered blandly.

"Don't you think it would be a good idea for me to have it if I'm going to care for Yulia?"

"I have no instructions about that."

I knew at that point I wasn't going to get anything out of him that wasn't part of his "instructions" and I had no intention of doing battle with him. Yuri would have to talk to him about giving me some leeway. How could I be spontaneous with Yulia, if I had to clear every outing with Brain? Obviously, I needed some limits, but I also needed Yuri to trust me. If I couldn't get that, well, I wouldn't last as a nanny no matter how much Yulia wanted me to stay.

Brain turned me over to the housekeeper, Mrs. Margot Henderson. She was the female counterpart to Brain in the facial expression department. Margot's face looked as if a smile might break it. She nodded stiffly and immediately took me on a tour of the house. There appeared to be no one around and our footsteps were loud on the polished floors.

It was the second time I was seeing it, but one did not simply get used to the grandiosity of such a house. Unlike the previous day though, I could now soak it all in. At the pillars soaring up to the innately carved ceiling, the red runner carpet on the marble staircase, the elegant chandeliers that flowed down like waterfalls of shining light. Every crystal confirming in my mind, if there had been any shred of doubt, the incredible wealth of the owner.

If Yuri wanted people to think he had money, he had definitely succeeded. Everywhere I looked, I found nothing but grandeur and beauty. Unique works of art and massive paintings filled the walls. From the grand piano to a massive library filled with books from floor to ceiling, the house was magnificent. Margot kept up a running commentary. After the orangery, which was breathtakingly beautiful, I was shown to a heated swimming pool. I gasped at the walls which were floor to ceiling aquariums filled with colorful fish. I wondered what they would be like at night when the lights were on.

I noticed I wasn't taken to Yuri's office and I wondered if he was even home. I didn't really care. I was here to take care of Yulia and if I could find out why she had stopped speaking.

I met the butler, Mr. Boris Orlov and some of the staff. There were at least fifteen, and there was no way I could remember all their foreign names or faces.

The kitchen was modern and spacious, and I was introduced to the Chef. I could only hope his cooking was considerably better than his almost hostile demeanor. Did Yuri take tea? *None of your business, April.*

As we passed a set of double doors, Mrs. Henderson nodded toward them and informed me that they led to Mr. Volkov's suite a floor above.

I showed no expression, but my mind started imagining all kinds of things. What was behind those doors? A ten-foot bed, five feet off the floor? A gold tub? More silk shirts than a Savile Row tailor? The latest music system?

In a way, I wished I could see, but then again I really didn't want to know if there were mirrors in the ceiling, or cameras in the corners. The thought made me shudder. Yuri wasn't above forcing a kiss on a woman. No, better I didn't know about his lair.

I had a horrible thought then.

What if he brought his women back here and I was forced to meet them or converse politely with them. I shuddered at the thought. I didn't feel like admitting it even to myself, but the disturbing truth was I was wildly jealous of any woman who might touch Yuri.

# CHAPTER 7

## APRIL

Eventually, I was shown to Yulia's room. The young girl lived in a suite of rooms. Her bedroom was designed for a princess, and somehow that felt totally appropriate. She also had a closet; hers was filled with many formal designer clothes. There was an activities room filled with toys and books. In the room was everything I would need to teach Yulia. Desk, whiteboard, books, a laptop. In one corner, I noticed a keyboard and I wondered if Yulia played. Music might provide a way to break through the girl's silence.

"Where is Yulia?" I asked.

"She is attending classes downstairs. You will meet her later."

The tour ended in my bedroom.

"Mr. Volkov wanted you to lodge just down the hallway from Yulia," Mrs. Henderson informed me.

The room was everything I could have ever hoped for. Tall windows invited in the blue skies of the elite neighborhood and the charm of London. A huge bed with lots of pillows, a heavenly Jacuzzi bath almost as big as the bed. A cream and gold walk-in closet that I could have happily moved into. My few possessions were going to look very sparse in there. There was a desk by the window that provided a lovely view of the garden behind the house.

I could see that Brain had already deposited my bag next to the door.

"I will leave you to unpack. Zelda, Mr. Volkov's Head Personal Assistant will be along shortly with your schedule."

I thanked her and she slipped away quietly. For a while, I did no more than sit on the luxurious bed and breathe in the sheer elegance of the space and the dreams that it promised.

It didn't take me long to unpack. I reasoned it would make my getaway easy if necessary and if I needed more, I could always return to my apartment and get more. As I hung my clothes up, I sort of regretted that I didn't bring at least one elegant dress. Just in case, I had to take Yulia somewhere formal. Everything I had packed was work clothes. No seduction wear since I was pretty sure I would never be able to seduce him, anyway. He seemed like the kind who took what he wanted.

I would have to keep in mind always that I was hired help, nothing more. I hoped Margot was on my side, and if I were lucky maybe in time, I would get the nod from Brain too. He seemed like a tough nut though.

The knock on the door was brisk.

"Come in," I called, running my hands down my skirt.

A woman of indeterminate age, she might have been sixty or forty, stepped into the room. Her ramrod-straight, thin body was clothed in a beautiful olive-green suit and a baby-pink blouse. While the clothes were expensive and fashionable, they didn't soften her appearance in the least. The severe spectacles only reinforced the image. She reminded me of a fairy tale character. Like a wicked witch in disguise.

"Good afternoon, April," she began in a heavy Russian accent. "My name is Zelda Popov. I wasn't here to meet you on the day of your interview and that is regrettable, since I am in charge of this house, everything, and everyone in it. As it pertains to you, my job is to make yours easier. I do not live here, and I am not always on site, but I will give you my mobile number, so you can reach me at any time. When you have requests, and you will, you must contact me."

"I'm very pleased to meet you to, Ms. Popov."

"You may call me Zelda," she said with a wave of her bony arm.

"Thank you," I murmured.

She took a few steps towards me and held out a folder. "Here is your copy of your contract, NDA, and your schedule. It is a simple one. Yulia has tutors, so your responsibility is only to take care of her. Make a list of whatever supplies you require, and I'll see that it's filled."

"I will."

"You can have Monday or Tuesday off. You are free on Sundays too. If you wish, you may join Yulia at church, it's Russian orthodox, but you are not required to do so."

"I'll have Monday off and I'll decide on Church later."

She nodded. "I will let the other staff know. Now meals.

Breakfast is served at eight, lunch at noon, tea at four, and dinner at seven. You will eat with the rest of the staff after Yulia has eaten, or you may decide to eat with her. This week's menu is attached to the file so you can peruse through and if there's anything of concern, or something you desire then just let me know so I can make the adjustments."

I glanced down at the plan of scones, chicken, and pudding, and felt my heart warm considerably. "Everything looks great as is, and I'm allergic to nothing."

"Good. Yulia is currently not attending school, but her afternoons are packed with tutors to ensure that she doesn't fall behind with her school work. Her uncle prefers that she arises early to begin her day. He is a morning person, so he prides himself in instilling that habit into everyone else around him. Please ensure that she is up and dressed and has had her breakfast by seven-thirty in the morning."

"Sure."

"Yulia loves to read," she continued, "So after breakfast she will dally in a book or two until her tutor arrives. After that, piano lessons followed by martial arts lessons."

I did a double take on that, wondering if I had misheard correctly, but no, it was clearly stated in the schedule. My eyes were filled with questions for Margot.

"Self-defense takes precedence over most things in this household," she explained. "Her uncle insists on it, even for you."

"Me?"

"Yes, I think you will find the lesson quite easy. As they will be basic maneuvers to ensure you can protect Yulia in the event of a mishap."

Why were mishaps expected, I wondered. Apart from their incredible wealth, and security, the household appeared quite normal and thus far, all I knew of the source of their good fortune was a family business.

"You'll get settled in no time," Zelda assured me.

"I'm sure I will."

I have been asked to inform you that you will be dining with Mr. Volkov tonight. I believe he wishes to hear if the facilities meet your expectations."

"I am more than happy with everything so far."

"Good you can tell him yourself." Zelda paused and pushed those severe glasses up her nose. "I wish to welcome you to the house. I will do whatever I can to ensure your success. I am on call twenty-four hours a day, so all you have to do is ask."

I smiled despite myself. While Zelda didn't look like a ray of warm sunshine, she seemed to have a heart somewhere inside that tailored suit.

"It's almost lunch now, so I'll take you to see Yulia and you can have your first meal together. I believe you have already informally met her."

"Yes, I have and that will be wonderful."

A few minutes later and I was shown to the dining room.

# CHAPTER 8

## APRIL

The six-year old princess was already waiting for me dressed in clothes that most other girls her age would prize as star outfits. She nodded solemnly to me.

She had an adult grace to her that I found almost disconcerting. I looked around at our surroundings. The whole room had been decorated with the kind of formal elegance that intimidated even me. The table was far too long and high for the child, the chairs too grand and heavy. The chandelier, well, it had more bulbs than a forty-foot Christmas tree.

"What do you think, Yulia, too much? Shall we find somewhere cozier?"

The little girl's eyes widened, then she nodded eagerly.

I turned to Zelda. "Can we move to that sunny room next to the kitchen? I believe there is a table there that's just our size."

Zelda frowned. "That is where the children of the kitchen staff eat when they come around.

"No wonder I thought it was perfect."

"Fine." She gave instructions in Russian to Margot who was hanging around at the entrance of the door. Her eyebrows arched, but she nodded and disappeared.

I led my charge into the bright little room with windows that overlooked an apple tree full of fruit. As we sat down, Yulia gave me a secret little smile. Lunch was chicken, mashed potatoes, and vegetables.

Yulia gracefully forked green beans and mashed potatoes in her mouth.

"You eat your vegetables so well," I said. "Do you like vegetables?"

She shook her head in response, and returned her attention to her meal.

"Then why do you eat them so well then? I mean it's amazing that you do, you need them to grow into a beautiful young woman, but it is unusual for a child to be so good about eating what's good for them."

She withdrew her notepad from the little pink purse she had slung around her body and began scribbling.

He

I was confused. "What do you mean?"

She didn't respond. She just went on with her meal,

sipping slowly from her glass of freshly squeezed orange juice. Her shoulders however, couldn't hide the weight her words held over her as they slumped forward.

This *'he'* was a concern for her, whoever it was. Whether that was positively or negatively, I needed to know. "Who is he?" I asked, but she didn't respond. She didn't even spare me a glance. So, I slid the notepad towards me and wrote my question down on it.

Who is he?

She glanced at it and then at me, and expressionlessly, returned to her food.

I felt as though I was speaking to an adult who seemed more in control of her emotions than I was.

Her sudden move away from the thrilled child that had smiled at me just a few moments ago to this coldly aloof creature troubled me deeply. I decided she needed more time. I moved back into clearer waters. "You have a free hour after lunch. What do you want to do?"

She came alive then, and wrote on the notepad.

Red hair. Like yours.

Her eyes pleaded with me to make it happen.

I knew instinctively that she was trying to manipulate me. Children are masters at that. It was obvious she had already asked an adult and been rejected so she was trying her luck with me. Normally, I wouldn't even consider coloring a child's hair, but I also understood it would be a bonding exercise for us. I needed her to trust me and let me get closer to her. I decided to think this one out. "I will see what I can do, okay."

The light died from her eyes as if she knew I would be asking the other adults and it was unlikely to happen, but she nodded anyway.

After lunch, I took Yulia to the activities room where we started a game of tic-tac-toe. While I expected to have to subtly, allow her to win, Yulia proved a bit of a champion at this game. For a six-year old child she seemed to have a natural affinity for spatial relationships and she won, or drew half the time.

After a while, I decided to do something else with her. We filled tumblers with water and I got her started on water color painting. Her painting tugged at my heart. It was a painting of three people in front of a house. The woman was wearing a pink dress and the man was wearing a blue shirt, and black trousers. They were both holding the hands of a little girl with curly brown hair. There were big smiles on all their face. A big yellow sun was shining and there were flowers next to them and behind them was a house with a red door. I assumed they were her parents, but I was careful not to ask about them. Something must have happened to them if Yuri was now her guardian.

Soon it was time for tea.

While Yulia listened, I spoke about tea and the British love affair with the afternoon ritual. I talked about where tea came from, how the different varieties were cultivated and graded. I told her about the tea picker in Sri Lanka. How the women tied baskets on their backs and went up the hillsides to pick the leaves. I told her that at every hour of the day and night, someone, somewhere was having tea.

By the time tea was over, Yulia had heard a great deal about tea and the history of tea, but she hadn't said a word.

I had once considered myself reasonably clever. I had never failed to entertain children and elicit squeals, laughs and chatter. From Yulia, I got nothing. The girl did smile once in a while, but she contributed absolutely nothing to the conversation, not even by writing on her notepad. I wasn't discouraged. I had never expected a miracle. Trust would be the key to unlocking the little girl's fear of speech.

By six, Yulia showed signs of fatigue so I fed her, ran her a bath, and read her a couple of fairy tales from one of her books. She smiled at me sweetly as I tucked her into bed. I wanted to hold her and kiss her vulnerable little face, but I knew I needed to give her some time, so I just smiled back and wished her a goodnight.

I went back to my room and found I still had time to have a shower and change before dinner. I walked my fingers through my limited wardrobe and gauged the sex appeal of the two dresses I had brought. Neither could be classified as a *come on*, which was a good thing. After that kiss and our agreement to keep it clean, I didn't want to give Yuri ideas. I settled on the black dress with the high neckline, then slipped into a pair of sensible flats.

It was just a casual dinner.

Nothing more.

## CHAPTER 9

### APRIL.

I headed down the marble stairs, my hand slippery with nervous sweat on the smooth banister. Dinner had begun about seven minutes earlier, but just as I was about to walk out of the door vivid memories of what had transpired between us the previous evening suddenly came back to torment me.

I felt haunted and unsure of my own convictions. I still hadn't been able to make up my mind about how I intended to deal with him, and until I did, I knew I was going to be vulnerable to his lure. Eventually, I forced myself out of my room. I'd never been a coward, and I wasn't going to start now.

Straightening my spine, I stepped into the vast dining room.

The silver shone, and the crystal glasses glistened under the great chandeliers. Yuri was already seated at the head of the table and smoking a cigarette.

My eyes skittered over to the other place setting at the other end of the table. The table was so long it seemed as if he was half a mile away, which would be a plus since his effect would be less potent.

"Come and sit next to me," he invited in that smooth, velvety voice of his.

I stilled. The much-needed distance from him I'd hoped for was fast disappearing. "If you don't mind," I began, unable to look directly at him. "I would prefer—"

"But I do mind," he cut me off.

In that moment, our gazes met. Blue curls of smoke rose around his dark face. His eyes glittered like ice and I felt as if there wasn't enough oxygen in the room. I found myself sucking in a big gulp of air. It seemed insane, but I had to admit to myself that in the mere space of a day I had missed him. The way his powerful personality affected me was incredible.

Almost unbelievable.

I'd hoped my memory of how strongly he affected me would be rendered inaccurate on second reflection as something that my mind, nervous about the job interview, had exaggerated.

I was wrong.

If anything, he appeared even more swoon-worthy. He must have just had a shower; his sinfully dark hair was damp and swept away from his brow, the top two buttons of his white dress shirt unbuttoned. The exposed, tattoos on the bronzed, toned flesh of his chest made my mouth go dry. His sleeves were folded up his arms. My eyes caressed the corded muscles of his forearms. There were intricate blue tattoos there too.

My gaze shifted up to his face.

A vein in his jaw popped and throbbed as he looked at me through the veil of smoke.

It held my attention for longer than was necessary. Was he as affected by me as I was by him? I couldn't pull my gaze away. It was as if my eyes needed to drink him in. It seemed almost indecent, this sexual attraction already brimming in the air between us.

He took one last drag of his cigarette and killed it in his ashtray.

Clearing my throat and holding my head up high, I walked to the seat beside him.

Orlov appeared out of nowhere, and with excessive politeness seated me and laid a napkin onto my lap.

I turned my head and looked at Yuri. Our eyes locked. It was like looking into the devil's eyes. For a few seconds, I became lost in his gaze. I got a sensation as if I was on my hands and knees crawling around on the floor searching. Searching, for my lost heart or soul. It brought back the lines from an old poem:

*You remind me of eyes I've seen before.*
*Eyes I'll always love.*
*Eyes I'm afraid of.*

A noise of cutlery shook me out of my trance and I hurriedly dropped my gaze in confusion. What was happening to me? Why was I so out of control? Did this man possess some kind of magic or was I just losing my mind?

I drew a ragged breath to steady my nerves and his scent filled my senses. It commanded the hairs on my arms to attention. Truly, I hadn't lied when I told Charlotte I could smell this man's desire for me. My mind felt restless and my body fevered. I stared straight ahead, as Orlav reset the place setting in front of me.

"Red or white?" he asked from my side.

"Red," I replied, and my voice sounded raspy, out of control.

Expertly, he filled my glass with wine from a decanter.

"Thank you."

Yuri lifted his glass in a toast. A slow, knowing smile lifted the corners of his sensuous lips. "To our health."

"To our health," I whispered. I tasted the wine, which must have been excellent, but it could have been water, all I knew at this moment that it was wet. I peered at him over the rim of my glass. "I apologize for being late."

He smiled a perfect smile and he lifted one side of his broad shoulder nonchalantly. "It is the prerogative of a beautiful woman to make an entrance."

I felt my cheeks burn with ridiculous pleasure at the compliment. "Thank you." Beneath the table, I made sure to keep my knees away from his and on the table top, I avoided any sort of contact with his hand. It looked dark, masculine, and lazily powerful resting on the snowy white table cloth.

I knew there was only one way this night would end if I didn't take matters into my own hands and lead the evening the way I wanted it to go. I took my slightly trembling hand away from the table and clasped them on my lap. "Yulia is a lovely girl," I began. "Talk to me about her. What happened to her parents?"

"They died a year ago," he said abruptly. His eyes were suddenly like cold stones. Flat and utterly dead.

I thought about the little one's drawing and my heart ached for her. I lost my mother when I was six, so I knew how painful losing even one parent could be. "I'm so sorry to hear that."

He nodded distantly, but his fingers were gripping the stem of the glass hard enough to break it.

I could see he didn't want to talk about it, but I had to know as much as possible if I were to understand what was going on with Yulia. "How did she take it? Did she comprehend that they were gone forever?"

He sighed. "She's never once asked for either of them from the moment I told her about their passing. She's a child but sometimes she seems as aware as an adult."

I nodded in agreement. "I sensed that while spending time with her today too. She chose the questions she wanted to answer."

"She wasn't always like that. Once she was very close to me. She used to wait for me to come to her house and take her in my car. I would draw back the sunroof and let her stand on the seat. She loved it."

"She doesn't do that anymore?" I asked.

"No. She's only interested in solitary activities now. Reading, drawing, playing games on her own."

"Right. Her parents died a year ago, but Yulia stopped talking six months ago?"

He frowned. "Yes. It happened while I was away on a business trip for four days. When I left she was talking normally, but by the time I returned, she had completely stopped talking."

"Did something happen while you were away?"

He shook his head. "Not according to my staff. They claim, and I believe them, nothing extraordinary happened while I was away. Yulia just woke up one morning and had either lost her ability to speak, or decided for whatever reason she no longer wanted to. I'd thought she was playing at first, but as time went on..."

"And it's not anything physical?"

"It was the first thing I checked out. All the necessary tests have been done. It's not her hearing or anything physical. All of that's perfect. Her psychologist called it delayed trauma, which if she wasn't the best in her profession I would suspected was something she made up on the fly."

He paused, creases in his forehead.

"I guess that analysis would have made sense if Yulia hadn't had a grieving period. That isn't the case. She cried and it took many months for her to come out of her shell, but she did. She was improving day by day, and moving towards a place of acceptance and all of sudden, boom, she turned silent. I've tried enticements, including a trip to Disney World, but nothing I offered made any difference. She refuses to engage in any meaningful way. Sometimes, she gives me the impression she is waiting for something to happen."

"Her parents...was it an accident?

Again, his face became a hard mask. "I don't think that matters. Bringing it up will only cause her more pain."

The curtness of his reply both surprised and stung me. I tried not to take it personally. As my employer he had simply reserved the right to withhold information as he deemed fit, but by his unwillingness to talk about the issue made me certain their deaths was in some way connected to Yulia's condition.

Orlov and another waiter arrived at the entrance of the room carrying dishes. A shallow bowl of cream soup with a thin garlic bread baked in the shape of a net placed on top of it was put in front of me.

I thanked the waiter and picked up my spoon.

"Good?" Yuri asked.

"Yes, it's very tasty," I lied. The soup felt like warm mush in my mouth.

For a while, no words were exchanged between us, just the low chink of our spoons against the bowls.

"I hear you took Yulia to eat lunch in the room next to the kitchen," he said.

"That's right, I did."

"Why?"

"I thought this room a bit intimidating for a child and I wanted her to relax."

"I see, but she will have to eat here when she eats with me."

"Or you could eat in the kitchen."

"Indeed, I could, but then, Margot would know all my secrets."

"As if she doesn't already," I shot back.

Amusement glinted in his eyes. "Touché."

Before I could answer, Orlov arrived with the second course. Duck with raspberry sauce, buttered samphire and red potatoes. I must have relaxed a bit because I could actually taste the food and it was the most delicious thing I'd eaten. "What about school?" I asked. "Do you intend to send her? The interaction with other children could be valuable."

He folded his arms across his chest. The strain of his perfectly sculpted biceps against the white shirt instantly dissolved my train of thought and I had to refocus to listen to his answer.

"In her present condition it would be a punishment. I won't take the risk of the other children being cruel to her. Why put her through that after everything she has had to suffer? Besides, I'm confident Yulia will talk again. She just needs some time."

"What about outings? Do you take her to the museums and theaters?"

He frowned. "No, as I said before she hasn't wanted to go with me. But she might go with you."

"Of course, I will take her. Fresh air and bus rides will do wonders for her."

His expression was implacable "No public transport. You will be taken wherever you want to go by my security staff."

"Can I ask why you decided to get a nanny for Yulia? She has tutors for her educational needs and more than enough people to handle everything else."

"It was her psychiatrist who recommended it. This house is too full of men and she thought a woman's presence might help."

"I see." I studied Yuri as Orlov served us lemon dessert. He seemed genuinely clueless about his niece's silence, but more important he seemed devoted to making her better. For me, that meant a great deal.

"Do you have any special plans for her?" Yuri asked.

I spooned the dessert into my mouth. It melted lusciously on my tongue. "Perhaps, but I haven't yet worked out exactly how to tackle the invisible wall she has put up."

Orlov refilled our goblets, and left.

Unconsciously, I sucked the spoon as I thought about Yulia, but when I looked up, I saw how he watched me and I knew instantly that he was turned on. His face showed his desire and I felt a flare of triumph. I felt the same urge. A part of me wished he would pull me from my chair and bend me over the table.

Part of me.

My cheeks heated up and I knew I was in dangerous territory. I wanted to flirt with the man I had chastised for kissing me. My dessert was unfinished, but I pushed back my chair and stood. "Thank you for a lovely evening."

He stood. "I look forward to many such dinners with you."

"Well, yes," I answered hastily. Then, before I could embarrass myself, I turned away and willed myself not to run, but walk out of the room. I'd done enough for one night.

On my way to my bedroom, I stopped to look in on Yulia. She was fast asleep. Her vulnerable sleeping face tugged at my heart. From the first moment, I laid eyes on her, something about her had touched me. I made a silent promise that I would do my best to change her life. One way or another, I would get to the root of her problem.

As I readied for bed, I wondered what his bedroom looked like. I slipped between my sheets and closed my eyes. What was behind those double doors?

# CHAPTER 10

## YURI

https://www.youtube.com/watch?v=xvvAYd3X5kA
-There must be some kind of way out of here-

I sat back down and I watched her walk away. Her curving hips, that delicious jutted ass. An immediate jolt of arousal shot straight to my groin.

What was it about this woman that so effortlessly turned my blood to fire? I'd had so many women in my lifetime. They'd all met me on their knees. Eager to please, their mouths open, ready to swallow anything I cared to spurt.

Not this woman. Damn her.

The last thing I needed was to have her walking around my house flashing her wares while I lusted like some stray dog for her flesh.

Hell, I wanted to spread her across my desk that first morning. Even today, I had to pretend to enjoy my dinner when all I wanted to do was bury my face between her legs. Sure, she would struggle, but I would enjoy that as well. Because I'd know, it was only a pretense. She couldn't hide the flame in her eyes, the tremble of her hands... She had it as bad as I did, perhaps even worse.

She was very near to cracking. It would be interesting to see how long she could hold it in before she came to me. I would keep my cool and wait.

But sooner or later, I would be fucking her.

With a smile, I left the dining room. The heat she had stirred inside of me gnawed at my insides. My cock hung heavy and hard. I headed out to the pool to cool off, but twenty laps later, I was still thinking of spreading her legs and my dick was still as hard as a rock.

A groan of annoyance at my inability to control myself escaped me. Damn her.

I swam to the deep end of the pool. I always swam naked. With my back against the wall of the pool, I shut my eyes and fisted my cock. Her image rose into my mind. That plump mouth stretched around my thick head, those beautiful emerald eyes staring up at me as I fucked her mouth.

I gripped the pool's edge. I was already so close to exploding. I conjured up the scent of her cunt and just like that, I exploded. Growling like a beast I came, hot cum spurting from my cock, and into the blue of the water. Even in the midst of my climax, I heard it. A noise. Soft, but years of training kicked in. My eyes snapped open.

April was standing at the edge of the pool staring at me, her mouth slightly open, her eyes enormous with surprise.

My chest was heaving and my pulse was still racing. I let go of my cock, leaned back, and let my arms relax along the edge.

She seemed to come to her senses suddenly. Her cheeks flushed with color and she instantly spun away from me. "Oh my God, I'm so sorry, Sir. I didn't mean to intrude."

I felt no embarrassment whatsoever. More than anything, I was amused by the turn of events.

She, however I was sure was close to digging up the tiles and burying herself in the ground. She took an urgent step forward.

"Stop!" I ordered.

Instantly, she froze in place.

"Turn around."

She whirled around slowly. And lifting her chin, met my gaze boldly.

Fierce excitement shot through me. "Why are you leaving?" I asked, my eyes running down the loosely tied robe she had on. It reached the middle of her calves, exposing them. The water's reflection played patterns on her creamy skin.

Biting her bottom lips, she tightened her robe around herself. "I apologize—" she began.

I shrugged. "For what?"

She shut her eyes for a brief second.

I couldn't hold myself back. "For purposely walking in on me, or for not having the guts to go ahead with your swim?"

"I didn't purposely walk in on..." She stopped and looked away in exasperation.

"Get in," I said.

"What?"

"You wanted a swim. Go ahead."

She licked her lips, and looked uncertain.

"I won't touch you if you don't want me to. Unless you are afraid to get in the water with me..."

The seconds slowed and ticked loudly as I waited to see what she would do. When her hands moved to the knot to her robe and began to untie it, her eyes filled with defiance, I lowered my head in amusement. She was going to make me like her before I realized it.

I wiped the smile off my face and kept my eyes on her as she made her way into the pool. Her swimsuit was a matronly one piece, but it fired my blood in a shocking way. Instead of looking dowdy, it accentuated the swell of her breasts and made me fucking want to tear it off her. She didn't look my way which was a good thing given that my dick was now riding high up against my stomach, the shaft clearly visible through the water.

She got in at the opposite end, as far from me as possible and stayed in the corner treading water.

A few minutes passed before I spoke again, "Are you just going to remain there?"

"I'm fine here," she replied without turning around.

I chuckled under my breath. "You don't seem fine, little rabbit."

# CHAPTER 11

APRIL

https://www.youtube.com/watch?v=bhRuIqIy7Iw
Too Lost In You

B*astard*

It was all I could think about as I cowered in the corner of the pool, wondering what had possessed me to ignore the magnificent shower in my room and instead, head out to this.

I had just needed to cool down so I could get to sleep, and a quick swim which would have both exhausted and calmed me had held the sweetest lure, however walking in on him—in that way…

I couldn't breathe.

I shouldn't have come in.

*You should have just turned around and left, you idiot...*

I couldn't understand myself. Was my resolve truly to see and regard him as nothing more than my employer, or was I provoking the both of us?

I fought the image of him lounging in the water at the opposite end of the pool, watching me with eyes I could have sworn were burning holes through my back. The huge tattoo spanning across the left side of his chest. I wanted to trace the sculpt of those abs with my tongue. And of course... there was his cock. How Charlotte would howl when I told her just how big it was. He had a very sizeable one, and from what I could see, any woman should think twice about letting such a monster inside her.

Try as I might to put myself off of it the image of him fisting himself, and the growl that had slid from his throat was all that swam around in my head. It had turned the swollen bud between my legs into a painful ache.

I felt unable to take a swim, or move away from my little corner, so I decided to just to leave. Feeling like a complete coward and cursing my stupidity for not doing it in the first place, I took a deep breath and prepared to go.

Just as I was about to turn I sensed movement behind me. My whole body froze as he emerged from the water behind me.

Swallowing the scream that tore out of my throat, I spun around. His dancing eyes were mere inches away from my face. It drove me backwards until my back hit the wall of the pool. "M-Mr..." I couldn't even remember his name.

"Call me Yuri," he suggested softly, his eyes though were dark with desire.

The strength left my legs, and I must have begun to sink into the water because his hand slid around my waist, or maybe just because he wanted to. In this moment, I wasn't coherent about a lot. I just hung on to him as if for dear life. "You said you wouldn't touch me, Mr. Volkov," I said, my gaze seeing absolutely nothing as I stared densely to the left of him.

"Yuri," he reminded softly.

"You said you wouldn't touch me ... Yuri."

"I said I wouldn't touch you...unless you wanted me to."

"I didn't say I wanted you to," I protested weakly. The sensation of his strong hand curled around my waist did all kinds of crazy things to me. God, how I wanted this man.

"Didn't you?" he murmured.

My throat closed at the look in his eyes. I could only shake my head.

"I didn't want to hire you," he muttered.

I swallowed. "Maybe you shouldn't have."

"Why not?" he asked.

I turned my face away from him.

With a finger on my chin, he brought my gaze back to his. "Why not?" he repeated.

I didn't think he needed an answer to the question and he proved me right. He leaned in and with his lips barely an inch away from my skin traced my scent up my jawline and then down my neck, slowly, excruciatingly. I shut my eyes like someone possessed and then from nowhere heard his voice in my ears.

"Because you want to fuck me too?" With an arm around my waist, he slammed me into his chest, my breasts crushed to the hardness his body. He rubbed me against him.

Oh, God, if he did this long enough, I felt sure it would bring me to an orgasm, a shameless brutal one. One that would leave me with not a shred of dignity. Shaking my head, I willed the strength back into my limp body, and putting my hands on his hard chest, I pushed myself away from him.

He let me go. "Why do you deny what's going on between us? You walked into the dining room and my dick was instantly hard. And you were flushed red. So you feel it too. What exactly is holding you back?"

Angry with myself for failing to conceal my desire, and at him for blatantly pointing it out, I frowned. "You're wrong about me."

He didn't say a word…instead, he brought his face toward mine.

I shut my eyes and my heart pounded so hard in my chest I was sure he could hear it. I could feel his lips burn a trail on my skin as they traced along the line of my jaw. A barrage of raw primal need coursed through my bloodstream. Something very dangerous loomed about him. I could sense it from the first moment we met. Now, as his pure animalistic strength seemed to overpower me, I wanted nothing more than to be ravished by him, but I made one last desperate attempt to escape.

His hand shut out to the edge of the pool and blocked my exit.

I stared at the network of bulging veins running down the heavily muscled limb. In that moment I couldn't stomach it any longer, so I turned to him and lashed out, "If you want to fuck me so badly, then just do so and get it over with."

His brows raised and the hint of a smile tugged at the corners of his lips.

I realized he enjoyed mocking me. It angered me even further. I didn't even care if I got myself fired. I shot out my hand underneath the water, my gaze not breaking away from his and grabbed his thick cock. I heard the excited gasp escaping his lips at my hold, and it gave me that bit of confidence I needed.

With his other hand, he caged me into place. I watched him while seething.

His lips spread into a full wolfish grin. "You're coming for blood?"

My frown deepened. Spreading my legs apart, I drew his cock to me forcing his entire body along, and over my swimsuit, I stroked the wide head up and down the lips of my sex. My head fell slightly backwards as I moaned silently at the sensation. A dark coil of ecstasy unfurled in the pit of my stomach.

He buried his face in my neck, and nipped bruising kisses on my skin, his tongue shooting out to tease my pulse before he moved onward and plunged his tongue into my mouth.

I lost myself then, pulling violently at the crotch of my swimsuit. I was mad for him. I wanted him inside me. In that moment of madness, I forgot about protection. I forgot he was my boss. I forgot everything, but the overriding need to have him inside me.

"Do you need help?" he mocked against my mouth, when he saw that my efforts were ineffective.

I wanted to shut his arrogant mouth. So I let go of his dick, and threw my arms around his neck. Grinding my hips to his, I sucked on his tongue as if I was a giant tick feeding on him. I wanted to cause him some sort of pain, so I bit down on his full lower lip until I tasted blood. I smiled when it caused his body to jerk.

"So you want to play rough," he growled. Grabbing the V neck of my swimsuit, he ripped the material apart as though it were paper.

I watched in shock as my red swimsuit turned into two hanging pieces before my eyes. He tugged harshly on the straps around my shoulder and the slight burn of pain against my pussy deliciously hardened my clit even further.

He was a rough man, but as he tore what remained of the swimsuit off my body and reached behind to grab my buttocks underneath the water, I decided that I wanted his brutality. I wanted ferocious fucking from him. He crushed my hips to his as he dived at my breast, sucking a nipple into his mouth. I writhed my hips desperately against him when he took his revenge by biting me back.

Without warning, he lifted me up from the pool, and plopped my bare ass on the tiles. Goose bumps appeared on my skin as he grabbed my knees and jerked my legs apart.

"Fuck, April," he rasped, looking at my exposed pussy. Then he came for my cleft and covered my pussy with his mouth.

With my palms propping me up, I threw my head backwards, thrashing at the wild assault. *"Fuck,"* I cried, writhing my hips to his tune as he ate me up like a maddened, starving man. He nipped brutally at my bud, stroking relentlessly at the tip with his tongue and then reaching down to greedily lap up the rush of juices spilling out from his assault.

When his tongue dug into me, I wrapped my legs around his shoulders and grabbed on his hair for the sake of my sanity. "Yuri," I called out, but in the distance, I heard his phone ring. I didn't want him to leave me so I tightened my legs around him. I couldn't bear it... not until he got me off. I was so close.

"Fuck," he cursed and began to pull away.

I panicked. "Don't you dare!" I wailed, and began to ride my pussy up and down his mouth and face.

With both his hands on my hips, he stilled me, his hold as solid as iron. His lips curled with amusement. "I need to get that call, little rabbit. It's urgent. Keep your legs open. I'll finish you off the moment I'm done."

*Fuck you,* I wanted to spit out at him, but since a part of my brain was still working and could register his authority over me, I didn't dare.

He pulled my legs away from his neck, and caressed my mound with careless fingers. At my glare, he hoisted himself up, muscles rippling, and water sluicing off him, and crushed my lips in a brief kiss. I tasted myself on him, and it fanned the flame of my arousal even further. I had to hold myself back from shouting curses at him as he swam back across the pool to retrieve his phone.

He got to it before it disconnected. I watched as he responded, his deep, whisky smooth voice filtering over to me in the cool air. I could see his firm ass cheeks in the water, and it frustrated me to no end. I couldn't wait for him. I needed to touch him, to feel his skin on mine, his cock in my mouth. So, I slid into the water, tearing what remained of the scraps of my suit fully away from me, and headed slowly towards him.

I stopped midway across the pool as a curse rang out from his mouth.

"*What?*" he snarled. His tone was low and menacing and forced a trickle of fear down my spine. "Did he lose his fucking mind? I'll be there in twenty minutes. If any of you even move an inch from there before I arrive, you're dead."

I froze, unable to move from where I was.

I watched as he pulled himself up from the pool and strode away, naked, proud, and wildly beautiful, but without even a second look back at me. It was almost as though I'd been wiped away from his memory. Suddenly, I felt very cold and painfully naked, so I covered my breasts with my arms in the water. As I looked on the tears stung my eyes and I wondered how the hell I was going to make it through the house.

A few moments later, I almost sunk completely into the water when Zelda appeared, calling out my name. Never had I felt so much shame. I cowered into a corner, hoping to hide away from her.

She spotted me and came over. She placed a folded robe and

towel by the edge of the pool and smiled kindly at me. "Mr. Volkov requested this for you."

"Thank you," I said, unable to meet her eyes.

She turned around to leave and I clothed myself in the shame of his callous dismissal.

# CHAPTER 12

## APRIL

"He did what?" Charlotte yelled into the phone.

"It's not a big deal," I muttered, even though I would have had the same reaction if Charlotte had said the same thing had happened to her. But with Yuri it was different. We had this crazy thing.

"The hell it isn't," her voice rose angrily. "He left you fucking naked in his damn pool without even a word, or even a glance… the uncivilized bastard."

"I was pissed off too, but the truth is I was the aggressor. I stayed. I wanted him, Charlotte. I still do. And anyway, he doesn't owe me anything. We're not dating. It was just what it was…a crude meet, and—"

"You need to do the exact same thing to him… worse even," she cut in.

I sighed. "Is that really the best solution you could come up with?"

"There's no other way," she said. "Fuck him halfway to somewhere and then run off before he comes... let him see what that feels like."

"First of all, are you angry that he didn't finish me off, or are you pissed that he abandoned me?"

"Both!" she exclaimed.

"Alright," I replied, amused by her temper. "Well, I'm in a strange place. I feel no shame about what we did. It's like I'm not in control of my body when I'm around him."

"So he is allowed to treat you like trash?"

"Charlotte, I told you he had an emergency. Who knows what that phone call was all about? It did seem like a life and death thing. I mean his whole face changed. He almost became a different person."

"Get out of that house," she said. "You don't need that job, find something else. I'll cover your rent this month."

"Nope," I replied. "I've made up my mind to stay."

"What? Why?"

"Two reasons. For Yulia. It's not her fault I can't keep my hands off her uncle. I promised myself I would do my best to help her. Also I want him, Charlotte. Real bad. I've never wanted anyone the way I want him. And before you say anything, I'm going in with my eyes open. I know what he is. He's a cad, but it's okay, because I don't want to marry him or get serious. That would scare even me. I just want to have a completely sexual, brief relationship with him. When it's all over, I'll dust my feet off and be on my way."

She was silent for the longest time. "Do you actually believe what you're saying?"

"Yes, I do. Why shouldn't I have a torrid affair with him? Trust me, it will be hard to find a woman who says no to him. Anyway, don't people do this kind of thing all the time?"

"You're not *people*. You don't form emotional attachments easily, but when you do, it's usually strong enough to mess you up bad."

"I'm not going to form any attachment—"

"You don't know that," she interrupted.

"Charlotte, you can't wrap me up in cotton wool to keep me safe. Even if I end up getting hurt, I still want to do this. If I don't, I'll regret it for the rest of my life. Do you understand?" She didn't say anything so I sighed. "Look, I need to get ready now. Yulia has a big day ahead of her."

"Okay. Okay, I get the message. Go and have your fun."

We talked shop for a bit then, but just before the conversation ended, I brought up the real reason I was still on edge. "I don't know what he does for a living."

"Why does that matter?"

"He's a filthy rich businessman, but I overheard him say something strange on the phone yesterday."

"What?"

"Something like *'if any of you leave there, you'll be dead,'* or something close to that. It didn't sound like a figure of speech but a serious threat, if you know what I mean."

She went silent and I could just imagine her, scrunched up hair and furrowed forehead as she pondered what I was saying.

"There's also security everywhere in the house. I don't see them outright, but I'm aware of them… and cameras, they're everywhere."

"Well, he is wealthy, so the wealthy need a different level of protection…"

"Even so."

She sighed. "Just in case this call is being monitored, remember what I read in the tabloids?"

"Yeah, I remember. I'm beginning to think your tabloids might be onto something.

"Okay, now I'm even more serious about you leaving."

"It's all right. I won't be staying for long. I'll have my rendezvous and be on my way."

She chuckled. "You sound brutal."

"Well, so is he."

"That's my girl. Now you guard your heart Miss Winters. I don't want you to come crying to me, because I'll have to go there and chop him into pieces."

I smiled quietly in response. "I won't. I promise."

"Oh, before you hang up, how big is the man's dong?"

Heat ran up my throat and into my face. "It'll…um…take a few tries before he'll be able to slide fully in."

"Goddamn!" she squealed. "No wonder you can't wait to bang him."

"I'm hanging up."

"Have fun and do everything I wouldn't do," she teased and ended the call.

# CHAPTER 13

## APRIL

Half an hour later, Yulia and I were picking out her outfit for the day from her closet of seemingly endless clothes. She decided on a lemon-yellow pinafore, a frilly white blouse and sandals with yellow flowers on them.

Twenty minutes later, we were walking down the grand marble stairs towards the breakfast room. The beautiful hallway was bright with sunlight and I felt positive and uplifted until I saw Zelda coming towards us. A vivid reminder of how she had found me last night played in my head and I cringed with embarrassment.

She, however, behaved as if she could recall nothing untoward. "Good morning, April and Yulia," she greeted. "You both go over to the breakfast room and someone will bring your meals over in a second.

Both Yulia and I had toast, eggs and bacon. Yulia instantly dug into her breakfast.

I mentally ran through her schedule for the day while I ate. "Yulia, how well do you speak Russian?"

She looked up briefly from her meal to gaze into my eyes. As though convinced I was asking out of genuine interest, she took out her notebook and wrote on it.

Very well

"Could you say something to me in Russian then?" I urged.

She saw right through me, and rolled her eyes. After a sip of juice, she scribbled once in her writing pad.

Why? You won't understand.

For a six-year old child she had an amazing vocabulary and admirable intelligence. The benefits of private schools and one-on-one tutoring, I guess.

"I know I won't understand, but I just wanted to hear what it sounds like."

Before she could respond, Yuri appeared at the doorway. My spine automatically straightened and my gaze became fixated on a blob of unmelted butter on my toast. He took a seat opposite me. I could smell his aftershave.

His simple breakfast of toast and a couple of fruits was brought to him. Ignoring the food, he took a sip of his black coffee, and over the rim of mug, caught my eyes on his.

Instantly, I looked away. After mentally kicking myself for doing so, I turned fully to him with the blandest smile I could muster. "Morning, Mr. Volkov."

"Yuri," he corrected automatically. His gaze was on me for only a moment before it went over to Yulia.

This callous treatment zapped me with anger.

"Yulia, how are you this morning? Good?" he asked.

For a few seconds the little girl became as still as a statue. She didn't meet his eyes. Then she nodded quietly, and returned to her meal.

I wondered at her withdrawal. I'd expected her to be bright and preppy around her devoted uncle. Instead, she was the exact opposite.

It made me turn to watch him, and I was struck once again by just how handsome he was. This morning, his hair was brushed away from his face. At the reminder of the way my hand had pulled on the jet black mass the previous evening, a painful shot of arousal jolted me.

Yulia turned to look at me.

I smiled reassuringly at her before returning to my meal, but as I pushed food down my throat, all I could think about was him. The feel of his thick length in my hand, his mouth between my legs... And how he had so easily abandoned me in the middle of the pool.

I had told Charlotte that it was all right, it didn't affect me, but some part of me still felt hurt. I wanted so badly to get back at him. Right now, dressed in the striped blue vest of his suit... with his arms bulging against his crisp white dress shirt, I wanted to rip it all from him and have him growl out my name. I wanted him wrapped around my finger. The desire turned to an irrational rage inside me.

"April..."

His dark velvet voice cut through me, and my gaze slithered

up to his.

For a few moments, he didn't say a word, his blue eyes studying the silent fury in mine.

I felt as though he understood. As though he could sense exactly what I was feeling.

"What will you be doing at 4pm this evening?"

My heart jumped. "Yulia has her math tutor."

"Good. Leave her in Margot's charge. I'll send a car to pick you up."

"Why?" I asked.

His eyebrow lifted at the defiance in my voice.

After the previous night, he no longer deserved courtesy. He could go ahead and fire me if he wanted.

He looked away from me and to Yulia. "Yulia, would you excuse April and me for a moment? Ask Margot for a coffee refill for me."

I watched as the little girl slid out of the chair with a concerned look for me and took her exit from the room.

The fear in her eyes worried me so as I turned back to her uncle I asked, "Why does Yulia seem so afraid of you?"

"It's the usual reaction most people have around me. You on the other hand seem particularly hostile."

I took a long sip of my juice.

"Is this because of last night?"

I boldly met his gaze. "Last night? What about it?"

He let his fork clatter noisily to the plate, and leaned back against his chair.

My anger slowly began to flame the fire of desire for him that had begun from the moment he'd entered the room.

"I had an emergency," he stated with a sigh. "Do you think I wanted to leave?"

I looked down at my plate. Suddenly, I felt almost tearful.

"I apologize," he murmured.

"There's no need to. I'm a big girl. I can take care of myself," I said quickly. "Why do you need me at 4 pm?"

He answered without taking his gaze off mine, "I'm going to put a gun in your hands."

My brain sputtered to a stop. "What?"

"You need to learn how to use it. Just in case you and Yulia ever encounter any danger."

I looked away from him to process his words. Encounter any danger? What kind of danger could we possibly encounter, especially if we're going to be escorted by his burly body-guards at all times? Charlotte's warning came to mind. What was I truly getting myself into?

"Scared?" he taunted.

I returned my gaze to his. "No, but I would like to know what kind of danger we might encounter that would involve needing a gun?"

"It's just a precaution. I take Yulia's safety very seriously," he said before pushing his chair backwards and rising to his feet.

"I don't want to use a gun."

"Consider it an occupational hazard. You're the one who wanted the job," he reminded me. "You can quit at any time you choose."

He started to walk away but my mouth moved before I could stop it, "What about us?" I asked.

He took two more steps, and closing the door turned the lock. Slowly, he turned to me, the corner of his mouth tilted in slight amusement. "What do you mean?"

I shut off my brain, rose to my feet and walked to him, only stopping when my eyes were boring into his, my breasts almost brushing his chest. "You don't want to finish the job you started last night?" I asked.

His eyes were sparkling at my audacity. "Oh, I want to."

When I was with him, I felt no shame, no embarrassment, no timidity. "When?"

Every trace of amusement left his face then. The public mask of approachability disappeared. Replacing it was the man I suspected he really was…an infinitely dark and brutal beast. "Tonight," he answered. "After we're done with your training." Pause. "Are you sure you can handle it?"

"Handle what? The training, or you?" I retorted.

"Oh, I know you'll be able to handle a gun."

My response shot out of my lips before I could even think about it, "Well, I got a good enough taste last night. It shouldn't be a problem for me."

His laugh was dry and short. "Good." He moved to unlock

the door and leave the room.

If Charlotte saw me now, she wouldn't believe how I was taunting and provoking this guy. It was just not me. I didn't do this kind of stuff. I knew I was playing with fire, but I couldn't stop myself. "Can you?" I asked.

He stopped. "Can I what?"

"Handle me?"

He charged me in an instant. One moment I was standing in front of him and in the next, my back was slammed against the table, plates and cutlery were crashing to the floor, the front of my shirt was gripped in his fist to hold me in place. My hand searched desperately for the edge of the table and the rest of my fake confidence.

His gaze roamed hungrily over my jutting breasts as my chest heaved. His eyes were veiled. "Put your claws away wild cat. I don't think you understand what you want to get yourself into."

I found the guts to smile. "Make up your mind. Yesterday, I was a little rabbit."

He went along with my show searching my eyes thoroughly. "Be ready at four."

My hand shot out to grab his crotch. He was rock hard and my heart jumped at the incontestable evidence of his response to me. "I already am, let's fucking get this over with."

"Over? Ah, little rabbit. You have no idea." He tapped the table twice as the laugh bubbled from him. Without another word, he turned around and walked away.

The moment he left, I pulled myself upright and tried to stand, but my knees buckled under me. I grabbed onto the table to keep from crumpling to the floor. Still fighting to breathe properly, I looked up to see Yulia watching me from the door.

She looked as though she were about to cry.

This immediately snapped me back to the present. "Yulia," I called out.

For a few seconds she just stared at me, then she ran towards me. I got to my haunches and she burst into my arms. Her hands went around my shoulder as if she was trying to comfort me. I couldn't understand what was going on. "Sweetie, are you all right?"

She didn't answer, just gave an odd sobbing sound.

I leaned away from her and met her tear soaked face. "Don't cry." I consoled. "Why are you crying?"

Consoling her only made her cry even more. Her sobbing evoked emotions in me that I couldn't understand, and I felt the tears trickle down my own eyes. I realized that she pitied me. For some reason, she thought I'd been wounded by her uncle. We remained like that for a long while, neither of us saying a word until eventually, she let me go and I rose to my feet.

"What's the matter? Won't you tell me, please?" I begged, searching her reddened, unhappy eyes.

She only shook her head and as expected, didn't say a word.

I'd never been so confused.

## CHAPTER 14

### YURI

April Winters distracted me.

Distracted was a euphemism for what she was doing to me. Hell, I didn't know whether I was coming or going with this woman. I couldn't stop fucking thinking about her. Her soft skin. That taunting red mouth. Those fuck-me eyes, those legs. God, those damn legs. And her sweet pussy. It'd taken everything I had to walk away last night. And now instead of concentrating on what was happening in front of me, I was damn well fantasizing about her.

Before me was a circle of five men ramming their boots into a cowering fool. They were close to killing him, and in that moment, I wanted to allow it.

I knew they were waiting on me. Had it been under my late father's, or even brother's command, they wouldn't have needed to. They could have simply filleted him and presented their victim's heart in a silver box. I'm not into wet work. I don't enjoy it, and I believe it is the best way to end up behind bars. I'm not a sociopath... I'm a psychopath. But for the first time in a very long time wet work had become necessary.

A fresh burst of fury burned through me once again, I shot up from the metal chair, making it crash noisily to the floor.

It made them stop kicking the moron on the floor. He gave a low groan.

My back was to them, my hands in my pocket. "Any news from the hospital?"

"He's in a coma... The jump broke his spine," Ivan explained the state of the man this coward had almost sent to his grave.

I wouldn't mind, but he was the only one with the information I needed. Fucking fool. "You've awoken the cops..." I muttered with irritation. I turned around and walked to the man huddled on the floor. His face was a bloodied, unrecognizable mess. "Now they're going to keep their eyes on everything until all this blows over you fucking *dog*." There didn't seem a word brutal enough to soothe the anger I wanted to unleash on him.

I heard his dying grunts and felt nothing. He was a traitor. For a second, I saw Yulia's face when I told her that her parents were dead. My feet itched to kick his worthless body, but I held back.

He was nothing. Nothing. I would win this war. I would exact my revenge on all who betrayed me. One by one. There would be nowhere to run, nowhere to hide. It was only a matter of time. "Finish him," I said coldly and walked away.

Exiting the container, I walked briskly across the construction yard, and was at the makeshift shooting range in no time. Just before I picked up the gun, my phone rang.

"I have Yulia's nanny in the car, Boss," Valdimir said in Russian. "Should I take her to the head office or..."

"I'm at the yard." I ended the call.

I slipped a pair of earmuffs on and pulled up the command for the target. Supporting my outstretched hand, I shut one eye, and hit the target right in the brain. One by one. I shot twelve bullets into his brain before her arrival was announced. Some of that anger was still in me, but thoughts of April returned.

I felt my throat constrict in anticipation. I just knew right now, she was the one I wanted to see more than anyone else in the world. I wanted to touch her, smell her, hear her racing heart, take some of this tension of out my body by slamming into her. I thought of her bent over as she took all of me. Every fucking inch.

Just how high would that quiet voice of hers go when I finally had her? My cock twitched, I entirely missed the damn target. I put the gun down to get the blood back to my head.

I looked at the door. Where the hell was she?

A quiet knock sounded.

"Come," I said turning towards the door.

It opened, but it wasn't her. It was Alexander, my second in command, and best friend since we were in middle school. He'd clung to me from the moment I told him how dangerous my family was.

"How did your mom die?" our schoolmates had asked me.

"My father shot her," I'd answered dryly.

Some had believed me and fled. Others had labeled me sick in the head, but this yellow-eyed, Godzilla of a boy had seen something in me, and stayed by my side. Whether he'd believed me then or not, I would never know, but either way as the years went by, he'd refused to leave and I realized no one else in my life could strike that deep note of affinity I had with him.

"What's messing with you?" he spurted out in Russian, his eyes on the stray shot.

I let out a heavy sigh and picked up the gun once again. I pointed it at the silhouette. This time, I added a faultless hole to the rest I'd already shot through its head.

"Shit goes awry like this all the time," he reasoned. "Why are you so on edge?"

"No reason," I said, turning in time to see his eyebrows shoot up for the briefest of seconds, before he veiled his expression and studied me in silence.

It was at times like this when I hated him the most. I didn't need his intelligence and silence. I needed a fucking gorilla who didn't understand me so well.

The door opened again, but he didn't take his gaze off me.

Cursing him silently, I turned to watch April walk in. She'd changed clothes. She wore a white polo T-shirt and dark blue jeans. Her hair was pulled back into a ponytail and I could see the beginnings of a bruise on her throat.

I felt a jolt of possession. *Fuck, I did that!*

The door shut from behind her. She seemed unsure of what to do next.

Alex's gaze turned to her for a brief second, then back to me.

I tried to keep my gaze neutral.

"Hello," she greeted quietly, then turned to Alex, but seemingly without a clue as to how to address the fearsome stranger.

Alex scared the shit out of everyone. He had tattoos on his neck and face. And he was as big as a brick outhouse. He gazed unsmiling, at her.

For a moment, I pitied her. He would watch her until he'd seen what he was looking for.

Awkwardly, she avoided his stare by looking at me.

I turned away to pick up my gun. I needed to shave the edge off. "Pick a gun from that rack," I ordered, and fired off a shot.

She jumped in fright at the deafening bang.

When I turned to see her hand clutching her chest and the extent of fear in her eyes, it filled me with remorse for my stupidity. Why did I do it? Because I didn't want Alex to know? Because she was turning me into an addict for her body? I'd never needed anyone before. I wanted them, I took them and after I had them, I discarded them. I'd never felt this craving.

Aware of Alex leaning against the table in the corner, I filtered the concern out of my voice and asked, "Are you okay?"

"I'm not," she answered. "I don't want to be here."

I felt a sudden fear that she would leave. Maybe I'd gone too far… and the fear shocked me senseless. I never cared if a woman stayed or left.

"You need to fuck her hard and quick," Alex commented in Russian. "Get her out of your system, then dump her. She's the wrong sort."

His voice was like a bucket of ice dumped over my head.

With that, he rose to his feet and took his leave.

# CHAPTER 15

## APRIL

https://www.youtube.com/watch?v=0sw54Pdh_m8
She Drives Me Crazy

On my way to meet Yuri, I had run into what seemed to be a man who'd been beaten into a literal bloodied pulp being dragged carelessly across the concrete yard. I got a glimpse of his face. It was so battered his eyes were swollen shut and his mouth hung open. Actually, he might've even been dead. There was something heavy and inert about his body.

Utterly horrified and shocked, I could do nothing but keep putting one step in front of the next. Igor, Yuri's driver pretended as if he'd seen nothing. We marched across the courtyard. My heart kept pounding in my chest.

Good God, I'd just seen a dead man!

For the first time, I started really looking around me. I was in a massive construction yard somewhere out in the East End. We reached the building and Igor opened the metal door and let me precede him. We were immediately in a corridor. We walked along it. We passed one room where the door was open and I could a see cluster of men with visible weapons tucked into their pants, puffing smoke from their mouths, and boisterous tones of Russian from their lips in hearty, or heated discussion, I couldn't tell.

I knew only that they had pale dangerous faces.

Yuri's words the previous evening, the disappearing act, and the crazy-tight security around the house were already beginning to put images and ideas into my head that made my blood run cold. I'd been all mouth at breakfast, challenging a man whom I realized could quite possibly snap my neck in two with his bare hands, or more easily send one of these hefty Russian brutes I'd passed to handle the job.

But the gunshot. This was truly the last straw.

Somehow, without understanding a word of Russian, I knew Yuri's imposing companion had said something horrible about me. His coarse tone in the foreign language had reverberated through the room and scattered goose bumps across my flesh.

Yuri wasn't ordinary. I don't know about the Queen being a reptile, but in this case, the tabloids were right. The Mafia angle wasn't fake news.

When the Russian man left, he turned to me.

"Why?" I asked simply.

"I'm sorry," he whispered.

I could see in his eyes he was sincere, but like he almost didn't know how to say the word. Maybe it was something people in his world did to people in my world just to see how we would react. It was a big risk. I could have gone to the police.

Whatever. I knew though he wasn't going to snap my neck in half with his bare hands. Just like that, I felt the fear in my soul begin to dissipate and in its place, came the charge of primal desire that strung up my body without fail every time I came into his presence. It made me want to claw up along his torso and hang on for dear life... My bare breasts against those pure slabs of muscle that was his chest, his cutting blue eyes on mine, and my tongue in his mouth.

I shook my head in wonder at the new direction of my thoughts. How could I feel like having sex when I'd just seen a dead body? I must be going insane. This was madness. Wrong. All wrong. I needed to leave. And I had to leave now, before I became this unrecognizable person who got turned on after seeing a dead body. I should have just kept walking that day. But I will this time. This time I was serious.

"April," he called.

I didn't even look at him. I just put one foot in front of the other and kept going. I was leaving and nothing, but nothing would stop me.

Until the gun went off. He shot me!

I *screamed,* but whether it was all in my head, or sounded in reality, I couldn't tell. My heart collapsed into my stomach. My hands rushed to my ears and my entire frame shivered in mind numbing terror. I felt certain that a hole had been bored somewhere through my body. I waited and waited to feel the pain, or perhaps feel nothing at all as I slipped into unconsciousness, but when I opened my eyes a lifetime later I saw the hole he had blasted instead through the concrete wall near where my head was.

I spun violently around, in such a rage that the tears spilled from my eyes. "Are you fucking out of your mind?" I screeched. Still reeling from the slam of my heart against the walls of my chest. I charged him. The shock and terror rendering me incoherent even as I shoved him violently. When the joint of one wrist twisted on contact with his rock-hard chest, and with no effect whatsoever on him, both of my arms shot out and attacked him, instead. He allowed me to rain blows on him until I slammed his back into the wall, my chest heaving with uncontrollable fury.

Effortlessly, he grabbed and held down both my hands. "Enough. Calm down. I wasn't shooting at you," he said, his gaze sharp, but his expression stoic and unreadable.

I knew I must be an unsightly mess. "Let go of me. I'm calm now," I said through gritted teeth.

He let go of me and I struck a slap across his face. The sound reverberated as loud as the gunshot earlier. It was as though the time froze. I glared at him, until the madness left my blood, my senses came back and the reality of what I'd just done set in.

My hand covered my mouth in shock as I gazed at the imprint of my palm on his skin. "I-I didn't mean to do that. I'm—I—I..." I tried to say, but it was as though I'd forgotten how to speak. I stepped back in fear, sure that whatever happened, I wouldn't leave here unscathed for what I'd just done. Then I turned around and sprinted for the door, but before I got more than a stride away, I felt a painful hold around my waist.

It lifted me clear of the floor, my legs, thrashing in protest.

“Let me go!” I cried, but everything was silenced when he turned me around and crushed his lips to mine. My body was pinned tight against him. My legs were off the floor, my neck twisted to accommodate his wet hot beast of a tongue as it plunged into my mouth. I should have bitten it, but like Pavlov’s dog, I sucked on it automatically, shamelessly.

His kiss tasted like heaven and hell at the same time; lovely, life-giving heat and the coldest of chills. I couldn’t bare for him to stop, but at the same time, another part of me stood and watched in astonished horror, wishing he had never placed his mouth on mine. I began to push against him, but came to the conclusion that my resistance was all in my head rather than in my actual limbs, since he didn't seem to be stopping and neither was I.

I turned in his arms when my brain eventually shut down and chased the thrill, chased the fire, and allowed the most delicious man I had ever tasted to devour me.

The breath was knocked out of me as somehow, my back ended up against the wall. I took great, big gasping breaths when finally, he broke the kiss and buried his face in my neck, his lips, tasting, nipping, and sucking at the tender skin there. I held on to his shirt for dear life, not sure if I was pushing him away or trying to find a way to somehow submerge myself into him.

“You bastard,” I heard myself say, memories of the fight floating somewhere amidst the mix off maddening euphoria.

"I'm sorry," I heard myself apologize thereafter. I was sure I had lost my mind.

His lips returned to mine, and I lost all coherence again.

The next thing I registered was his hands violently tearing at the button of my jeans, and I needed them to be off as much as I needed to take my next breath. His mouth found its way to my breasts, taking in as much of the plump mounds as he could through the material, but I needed more. I ripped the T-shirt over my head ripped away my bra, and with my hands around his neck slammed his face back into my breasts. It was such a disrespect to my own body that I wondered if I would ever be able to forgive myself. But I couldn't stop. All I needed was him—in me and everywhere around me.

As one hand plumped at the breast, I'd thrown at him, his mouth was on the other, sucking and nipping at my swollen nipples. He slipped his heavy hand roughly into my panties and grasped at my mound.

I felt his fingers slide into my dripping wet pussy and for a moment, felt my heart stop. He squeezed the soft supple flesh hard and I felt myself unravel.

Jesus. What was happening to me?

It all terrified the hell out of me. This wasn't supposed to happen. This man was too dangerous. A criminal. I let go of his neck and began to push him away. "No!" I cried frantically, and closed my hand around his wrist to pull him away, but he wouldn't budge.

"Games, wild cat," he mocked, as he slipped another finger inside of me, and then another.

I felt my bones begin to melt. His fingers thrust expertly in and out of me, rapid, and fluid, while I writhed my hips in a crazed trance to meet his onslaught.

Time passed or stopped, I couldn't tell, I only knew sensation, the waves of pleasure radiating from his fingers through my whole body. I came hard, hugging his head in wonder. All he'd used were his fingers and I'd been close to losing my mind. I pulled away from him to stare into his eyes. How stupid I had been when I told Charlotte I would merrily walk away when this was over. This would never be over. Not for me. What male would ever live up to this? Now, I knew I wouldn't be able to survive this man.

"We have to stop," I whispered.

"Why do you keep trying to run away?" he asked. "I haven't even started with you."

I couldn't respond. Instead, I began to push away, from him, frantic for him to let me go.

"No," he snarled. "Not before I've had you." Grabbing both the waistband of my panties and jeans, he tugged them down my legs. Lifting me off the ground, he kicked away the crumpled clothes.

I was standing buck naked in front of him.

With a groan, he dropped his head and sucked on the wildly throbbing pulse at my throat. While I was distracted by the sensation, his lips completely possessed mine again.

I was nothing but a wimp against the wall.

Without thinking, my thighs spread open when I felt the rock-hard shaft he pushed at my entrance. He stroked the thick head up and down my swollen, soaked sex. Like an animal in heat, I lifted my leg and held on for the ride.

Lowering himself slightly, he plunged into me.

Jesus Christ. It took my breath away. My eyes were jammed shut, as the euphoria of the kind of fiery, livid lust I'd never known completely possessed me. I heard a groan.

Whether it came from him, or me I couldn't tell—not that I cared.

Yuri Volkov *fucked* me so hard my legs completely left the floor. His cock ramming brutally and ceaselessly into me. I couldn't match his thrusts. Neither could I keep up with his hunger or virility, so I just wrapped my arms tightly around his neck and hung on, as tears rolled down my cheeks for a second time that evening.

He swore in Russian, while I pulled on his hair needing to vent at his delicious assault.

To my shock, I climaxed again. This time it was like an explosion. As Charlotte would say, 'un-fuckin-real'. As my pussy convulsed around his thick cock, my entire being shuddering uncontrollably.

It tipped him over the edge and he joined me.

Together, we groaned, grunted and fought to catch our breaths. The first time he made me come, it had been easy to remain soundless, but with the fragments of my senses that I still had a hold on, it registered that I would most probably have trouble speaking or even walking for the next few days. I felt bruised all over and violated, in the most delicious way I could've ever possibly dreamed.

My lips glided across his face in search of his mouth, and I kissed him, deeply, afraid that this moment would never come again. He allowed it and then I felt his thick cock slide out of me.

I was leaking, both his juices and mine, and it was the most erotic thing I'd ever felt. Oh God, I'd let him come inside me! I panicked and held on tighter refusing to break the kiss or my hold. Just wanting to pretend everything was okay. I could stay in this room like this forever.

He was the one who pulled away.

I was too afraid to open my eyes.

Silence grew between us, and when it became too painful to bear, I brushed my sweat dampened hair across my shoulders, and without looking at him began to arrange myself in order. The walk of shame just started. I picked my panties off the floor. If he apologized, or if he said this was a mistake, or if he said we could just pretend this never happened, I swear, I would kill him in his sleep. But he didn't say that.

"I didn't take any precautions" he stated, his voice strangely hoarse.

My gaze flew to his face.

He looked actually a bit shocked, as if this had never happened to him either. He shook his head. "I had a condom in my pocket, but I didn't think to use it."

"It's okay. I'll take care of it," I said quickly, and pulled my panties and jeans back in place.

I saw him reach for me and I was suddenly so alarmed, I

moved out of the way. Our gazes met and I could see the anger in his.

All he'd wanted was to help me.

"I'm fine," I said, and focused on straightening my T-shirt. I listened as he arranged himself and pulled up his trousers. I couldn't meet his eyes.

Towering quite considerably over me, I felt his shadow looming over me.

"You'll still have to learn to shoot," he said, before exiting the room, shutting the door behind him.

Only then, did I lift my head and let out a strange wail of bewilderment.

## CHAPTER 16

### APRIL

I dragged my luggage down the stairs before anyone else awoke, and hid it in the closet by the foyer. Exhausted from a night of sleep deprivation, I spent most of the night worrying about how I would tell Yulia I was leaving. I'd promised I would stay and help her. I knew she was frightened about something, but I just couldn't keep my word. Yuri was devoted to her and he would eventually find someone else to help her.

I straightened and wiped the sweat away from my brow.

My heart jumped when I heard a sound behind me. I spun around and to my horror, Yuri and his immense and rude companion were watching me, their hands in their pockets. They were magnificently dressed, clothed in tailored luxury suits I was sure cost more than everything Charlotte and I owned. There must be cameras around the house. They must have seen me creep down the stairs.

I met Yuri's eyes boldly, refusing to cower.

He didn't say anything, but his cold stare was a demand for an explanation.

"I'm leaving," I declared, lifting my chin. "I'm sure you'll agree that it's not a good idea to remain in this house." My words sounded borderline silly, but I didn't care, they could think what they wanted.

Yuri continued on his way without a word, and I was left staring after him in shock. He didn't care whether I stayed or went! Something inside me broke.

"You can't leave," I heard his companion say.

I dragged my gaze back to him. "What?" In truth, he intimidated me. He was the kind of man I would cross the street to avoid.

His face looked stern. "We have business in Positano, we'll be back in two days, so please remain with Yulia until then."

"I—"

"It is important. Do it for the child."

I nodded.

"Thank you," he said with a nod, then walked off too.

I was left staring after both of them, as the gigantic front door banged shut. The sound seemed to shake the house... and my heart. I felt so on edge, and unsettled. A dark cast of sadness overcame me and I was left with the hollow feeling of a reeling, cold loss. I really was just a fuck toy for him. I'd given myself so easily too. I felt like a slut. Something a rich man had used and discarded. My only use now was as a nanny for his niece.

Fine. I comforted myself by reminding myself that this was what the devil did. He made us do the unthinkable. I would stay for those two days and then I would go. Fortunately, my heart wasn't broken. Only my ego had been dented and only a little. I was a fool, but everyone made mistakes. Yuri would go down in history as my greatest mistake.

Never again, would I let a man take me down this path.

# CHAPTER 17

## YURI

*I'm sure you'll agree that it's not a good idea to remain in this house.*

What the fuck! I was so fucking furious, I actually saw red. I couldn't think. I couldn't speak. I just wanted to throw her over my shoulder, march upstairs, and fuck her until she came to her fucking senses.

But I didn't have that luxury. I couldn't fuck it all up, because my dick wanted pussy. The only thing I could do was walk away. I knew to even attempt to call her out on her bullshit would have only made it worse. Irretrievably worse.

She intended to walk away. Just like that. Well, fuck her. I didn't need her. What did she think? She was the only woman with a pussy between her legs? I could replace her in a heartbeat. And I would. When this shit was over, I would go out there and fuck twenty redheads until I got her out of my system.

This was for the best. I'd broken my most sacred rule. Never mix business with pleasure. I was getting too entangled. Last night, instead of concentrating on the plan, I couldn't stop thinking of her, and wanting to go to her. I didn't need this shit in my life. A woman was for fucking, pure and simple. Anything more and they got you by the balls. No woman was twisting me around her little finger.

Not April Winters. Not anybody.

I realized that Alex had stayed behind to talk to her. It made me even angrier to think of him talking to her. Did he want to fuck her too? I swallowed the ball of fury in my throat. Would she open her legs for him the way she did for me? My fists clenched, then opened when I heard his footsteps close behind me.

I wrenched the door open and walked out. It was already hot and balmy. I heard the door slam and Alex joined me on the steps. We didn't speak as we walked to the car.

I slid in as Alex got in on the other side. "I'll replace her," I said coldly.

"She's going to stay until we get back. Yulia needs someone to be with her," he replied.

I felt a jolt of pleasure run through my body, but I didn't say anything.

"But it is a good idea to replace her. I'll ask Zelda to start arranging new interviews."

I turned my head and looked out of the window. Alex was right. It would be the best solution. Replace her and get back on track with my life.

I had let things get too far.

Too crazy.

# CHAPTER 18

## APRIL

Yulia and I spent the afternoon on the floor of her massive, baby pink tiled bathroom.

To kind of make up for the bad news that I would soon have to break to her about leaving, I promised her an activity of her choosing after her lessons. Her immediate request had been to dye her hair color to match mine.

She was only a child and I really didn't want to use dye on her beautiful virgin hair, but I had an idea. I asked Zelda if she could get me some American red Kool-Aid. I had to spell it for her, but in less than an hour, she had located a supplier and got me the four packets I'd requested.

I gave little Yulia a choice. We could put the Kool-Aid on for an hour and her hair would be a little bit red or we could leave it on for three hours and it would be almost as red as mine. I warned her that three hours with a shower cap on would be annoying, but she was determined.

I thought she might cave in, but bullheaded determination

must run in this family's blood. She kept the Kool-Aid in her hair for the full three hours.

A batch of freshly baked scones courtesy of the Chef kept us company, as she sat atop the counter, and I blow dried her mid-back length hair. Her mouth was stuffed with the pastries and at the amused look I gave her, she smiled and offered me a bite. I accepted it, purposely nipping her hand in the process.

With an impish grin, she pulled her hand away, just in time to save it. I really liked this child. If only things had been different, I knew I could have gotten her to talk. With a sigh of regret, I turned my attention back to her hair, and her blue-eyed uncle.

I missed him, and not in a heartfelt way, but in a sexually frustrated way. My pussy felt hot and strangely swollen from the violent fucking Yuri had subjected it to and my body felt empty.

When I was done with Yulia's hair, I ran my fingers down the red mass and turned her around to face the gigantic mirror.

I'd expected her reaction to be joy or at least surprise at the new look, but when she stopped chewing and went quiet at her image…I was confused.

"What is it?" I asked.

Seconds passed and she didn't say a word. Then she smiled, but it was such sad smile that my heart broke.

"What is it darling?" I pleaded.

She began to cry.

I knew she couldn't be the adult she was trying so hard to be by masking her emotions. I wanted so much to help her, but I didn't know how to. "Please don't cry, my darling. I'm here for you. Just tell me what's wrong. Please. What is it? Maybe I can help," I begged as I pulled her into my arms.

But she wouldn't speak. Just cried her little heart out, her chest heaving with the choking sobs.

I held her tightly to my chest and waited patiently, patting her back to comfort her. I didn't know how I would be able to leave her in such a fragile state. Part of me began to think I couldn't do it. I would just have to stay away from her uncle and help this poor suffering soul. If I didn't help her I would suffer far more than, if I got my heartbroken by a cold, heartless man.

Lifting her from the counter, I carried her back to her bedroom and laid her on her huge Princess bed. Then for the first time, I fitted my body next to hers. Was it her inability to speak that hurt her or the loss of her parents that haunted her?

She had so much more than I ever did when growing up. I'd been bounced around foster homes until eventually I grew past the age of being wanted, or even being able to be adopted. Rather than being angry at the unfairness of life, I had just returned its chill and aloofness to everything and everyone around me without apology. Except Charlotte.

And now this poor little girl. I could almost believe that right now she was sadder than I'd ever been.

I cradled her in my arms and rested my head against hers. I knew from experience that the tears would probably be a good release for whatever demons were tormenting her.

Eventually, she quieted down. When she shuffled, and tried to pull out of my arms, I immediately let her go. Sitting up, I watched her.

She got off the bed and headed over to her chest of toys by the windows. She brought out a photograph in a gold frame.

I waited patiently.

She came over to me with it. I knew I was being shown into the world inside her head. This was very important to her.

With a great show respect, I took the framed photograph from her and looked at it. It was the image of a man who bore some resemblance to Yuri, but there was something weak about his jaw, his mouth or his eyes. I didn't know what it was. I only knew he wasn't Yuri.

He however wasn't what held my attention. It was the woman by his side. Yulia was the exact replica of her. The wind was in her hair. She was laughing, carefree. My heart took a dive into my stomach. I'd never seen Yulia laugh. Not once.

I was so engrossed by the photo that it was only when Yulia nudged me with her notepad, did I turn around to gaze into her eyes. I looked down at what she had scribbled down and the words seized my heart.

Mama and Papa were murdered.

"What do you mean?" I asked, shocked.

She opened her mouth as though she might speak, but suddenly she shook her head as if reminding herself not to. She took the photograph from me and returned it to its original place. Then she climbed into bed beside me and shut her eyes.

I understood what she was doing. She was deliberately closing the cruel world out. I could see tears slipping out of her closed lids. I let her cry. She needed it.

I waited until she was so exhausted that she fell asleep. I wished I too, could fall asleep and forget the world around me, but my mind wouldn't slow down. Then, I got up and called Charlotte.

# CHAPTER 19

## APRIL

"Yulia showed me a photo of her Mom and Dad," I said the moment she picked up.

"What?" she asked, her voice groggy with sleep.

"The poor child cried herself to sleep," I added sadly.

Charlotte yawned, and it was only then that I realized that she'd been asleep. My eyes darted to the clock on Yulia's wall. It was past three in the afternoon. "What's going on? Why are you sleeping at this time?"

"I'll tell you later," she croaked.

"Are you okay?"

"I am," she responded. "You're the one who sounds like you have the weight of the whole world on your shoulders."

"It's nothing. Call me back when you're awake, okay?"

"No, let's talk now," she said, alertness coming into her voice. "I won't be able to sleep otherwise."

My heart swelled at her boundless selflessness whenever it came to me. After what had happened with Yuri, it was just the warmth my bruised soul needed. She'd been this way with me from the first day we met. Inseparable friends.

I went straight for it. "I slept with Yuri last night."

Silence.

"Are you asleep or just stunned?"

"Umm..."

I could almost picture her rubbing the sleep out of her eyes.

"You actually did it?" she asked.

"What do you mean?"

"I don't know. A part of me thought you wouldn't. You tend to run away from things that are too threatening to your peace of mind."

"Well, you're not too far wrong. I packed up my stuff. Right now, my suitcase is in a closet in the foyer."

"As expected. Does that mean he was a disappointment?"

"The opposite. I'm still sore."

"*Damn*. A good fuck. So why the hell are you leaving?"

I gave her a half-truth. "He's dangerous Charlotte. I was at his company yesterday, and there were guns everywhere. I think I even saw a dead body too."

She was silent for a moment. "And?"

Her reaction shocked me. "Did you hear what I said?"

"Yeah. You saw a dead body."

"Exactly."

"What does that have to do with you? Your only business is with his niece. Are you that scared you'll fall for him?"

"I'm not going to fall for him."

"Okkkkay."

"You know what? It's fine."

"By the way, I did more research on your boss. He owns a conglomerate, according to good ole Google. Construction, Manufacturing, Real estate, investing. Cyber security. A whole host of other things and now, you tell me he can fuck well too. What I wouldn't give to be you right now."

"Uh, *well* is putting it lightly."

"Did you confirm his dick size?"

"Charlotte!"

"What? That was the main point of all this."

"I didn't," I said. "All I remember was the ceiling... It was green. "

"Still, you should be able to gauge it? Did you guys do it on a bed?"

"I was pinned against a wall."

"Damn, can I take your place? I think quitting is the right call to make. Recommend me as your replacement."

"Charlotte," I exclaimed, exasperated.

"I'm not joking."

"That's the whole problem," I replied.

She sighed. "Can you come back to the apartment, tonight?"

I was about to refuse, but then I thought why the hell not? I could take Yulia with me. See what Charlotte made of her. "It might be possible. He's away on a business trip for a couple of days, so I could come with Yulia. It will be a breath of fresh air for her." I paused. "There's security everywhere though. I don't think it'll be that easy. Let me think..."

"Circumvent them. Go out for ice cream or something, and lose them from there."

"Um, I know you're already excited by the idea, but these men aren't Mr. Hensen look-a-likes," I said referring to our lanky high school math teacher. "One of them could quite easily snap both of our necks at the same time."

"Uhh, that's murder."

"Exactly. It seems like something they could be quite easily provoked into doing."

She sighed heavily. "Get yourself and the little girl out of the house tonight. I'll meet you both at the place where we bought my red shoes," she said mysteriously. She was so into this spy shit. "We'll figure something out. Don't worry," she added.

"All right," I agreed, and the call came to an end.

# CHAPTER 20

## YURI

"How's Yulia?"

Two words. A simple question, but Brain hesitated, just a fraction of a second, but that was enough.

I stopped in my tracks, and turned around to glance at the thick-headed brute. His eyes darted nervously away, so I turned fully to face him. My heart felt like lead.

He cleared his throat. "We're sure she's all right, boss. The Nanny took her away last night, but they should be returning soon.

"What?" I bellowed.

He swallowed hard. "There is no reason why they shouldn't be returning soon," he repeated fearfully.

"Where did she take my niece to?" I asked refusing to believe my ears as I turned to watch Alex disembark from the plane.

Brain began to stutter out a response as I unbuttoned my

sleeves, and roll them up my forearms while my mind raced with possibilities.

Instinctively, he took a step back, but before he could take another, his heavy hunk of muscle and flesh body was on the tarmac.

My wrist throbbed painfully at the slam into his face, but before I could go after him again, Alex was on me.

The man stood to his feet unsteadily and with his hands held up as if to appease me, and stumbled off. The four others who had acted as our escorts made no move.

I jerked my arm free of Alex's hold, and while flexing my throbbing hand, I made for the waiting black Mercedes.

My chauffeur jumped out of the driver's seat on my approach, and opened the passenger door for me.

I slammed the door shut and slid into the driver's seat he'd vacated instead. The engine was running. I put the car into motion and screeched away from the tarmac.

I dialed April's number on my way, but just as I had expected, it was turned off so I set my GPS system with the address she had included in her resume.

It was an apartment in a rundown neighborhood in Hammersmith, and it didn't take me long to arrive. By the time I did, my temper was close to exploding. Yulia wasn't meant to leave the house without security! That was the one unbreakable law I'd given to the entire staff and they had broken it. And certainly not to a place like this where no reconnaissance had been carried in beforehand.

I banged on the chipped painted white door, and began to count to twenty before I damn well broke it down.

At count sixteen, it was pulled open and standing before me was a blonde with laughing cornflower blue eyes. She was a bit taller than April but looked no older. Her eyes widened when she saw me. "You're Yuri," she said, then shook her head. "I mean April's employer. Yulia's Uncle."

"Where's Yulia?" I barked.

"Down the hall," she said and jerked her head to indicate the location. "April's giving her a bath."

She stepped out of my way hurriedly at the same time that I barged in and barreled down the direction she had signaled.

"Hey, hang on a minute!" she called.

Ignoring her, I burst open the door at the end of the hallway to a picture that should have warmed my heart, but I was too angry to be reasonable. Yulia was squealing as April tousled her wet hair in a towel while laughing.

At my sudden arrival, both jumped in shock. "Yuri?" April gasped. Her eyes immediately filled with dismay.

This made me even more furious.

I turned to gaze down at Yulia.

She stepped behind April's legs, her eyes showed the usual terror that appeared in them whenever I was near. Her hair was bright red.

"What the fuck have you done with her hair?" I yelled.

"It's not hair dye. It's just Kool-Aid. It's perfectly safe," April rushed to explain.

"Get her dressed and in my car in five minutes," I said and walked away.

# CHAPTER 21

## APRIL

"He fired everyone!" Zelda exclaimed.

The strength left my legs as I lowered myself onto the couch and shut my eyes, my phone cradled against my ears. "How is that possible?"

"All sixteen of us," she said. "He's given us twenty-four hours to get out. I'm packing my things now. I'm so confused."

"He can't do that. I'll be right there," I said.

"I don't think you should come. I've seen him angry before, but never like this. It's a scary sight."

"Then what about your jobs?" I cried guiltily.

"There's nothing you can do either way. You're automatically fired too. The only person that could probably change his mind is Mr. Vasiliev."

"Who is that?"

"His best friend. You know that big guy with tattoos on his neck and face that's always around him," she explained.

Oh, yeah. "Do you have his number?"

"Of course, but I'm still bound by my NDA. I am not allowed to give it out under any circumstances," she paused. "Give me a minute, Anton," she said, referring to the aged gardener.

"Oh my God, did he fire Mr. Orman too?" I asked in shock. He was one of the few people I actually liked when I was introduced to the staff that first day I arrived.

"No. Not him. He's like a father to Mr. Volkov. He is the only one left and the security. The very ones who didn't do their jobs in the first place. No offense to you, dear."

"I am so sorry. He was meant to be away for two days. I didn't know that he would return so suddenly in this way," I cried, filled with remorse. "I'll find a way to fix this. Please send me Mr. Vasiliev's number."

Seconds later, I received the text message containing the number.

Charlotte was sitting on the couch watching me, a steaming cup of hot chocolate and marshmallows in hand. "I don't think I've ever seen you so bothered," she commented. "Calm down, will you?"

With shaky hands, I paced around our tiny living room as I waited to be connected to the giant's number. My heart slammed painfully against the wall of my chest when the ringing stopped. "Mr. Vasiliev? T-this is...er...April Winters. Yulia's nanny."

"Yes. What do you want?" he asked coldly

At his tone, my hope died on the spot, but I couldn't give up. Not until he told me no to my face and even then I wouldn't stop trying to sort out the mess I caused by my careless actions. "Could you please help me by speaking to Yu—I mean…Mr. Volkov. Taking Yulia from the house was my sole doing. None of the other staff were even aware. He can't make everyone suffer on my account." I could hear my voice begin to crack so I paused and took a deep breath.

"Why are you contacting me?" he asked indifferently. "I'm not the one who fired them."

"You're the only… I heard you're the only one he listens to."

"Yuri listens to everyone," he said.

For a moment, I was taken aback. Whether his words were bad, or good news, I couldn't tell.

"Now, if you excuse me, I have other matters to attend to."

Suddenly, there was nothing but silence on the other end.

I stared at the empty screen of my phone until Charlotte's voice pulled me back to the present.

"What did he say?" she asked.

"He said he couldn't help. That Yuri listens to everyone." I stared at her. "What does that mean, anyway?"

She gazed at me blankly, then grimaced. "That can't be good."

"What do I do now?"

She raised her eyes to the ceiling to think. "No one listens to everyone. Who is this guy? Is he as hot as Yuri? God, that Yuri is holy-moly-macaroni hot."

"Charlotte!" I nearly screamed. "Not now."

"All right. All right. Calm down."

"These bloody Russians. They are so freaking cold and unfeeling. They speak as if words cost money." I racked my brain for an answer. "What if it means just what he says? Not that he listens to everyone, but that he gives everyone a chance and then makes his own decisions?"

"Doesn't that mean the same thing?" Charlotte asked. "Since he is Russian too, maybe it's a second language thing."

"Yes," I said distractedly. "I can't see I have any other choice, but to go and see Yuri."

She smiled mysteriously. "Hmmm."

"What do you mean Hmm?"

"Nothing."

I shot her a dark look and hurried off to get ready.

# CHAPTER 22

## YURI

When I drove home with Yulia in the backseat, I should've been relieved, instead I was infuriated. What I really wanted to do was go back and take April into my arms. I wanted to scold her for being so careless and willfully negligent and…then punish her. The way I knew would drive her crazy. I wanted to whip her ass until it was as red as her hair and when it was burning with pain, I would fuck her so that every time I pushed into her she would scream with pain and pleasure. I wanted to see her spread open before me and begging me to use her. Not creeping down the stairs with her fucking luggage to run away.

I glanced into the rearview mirror at Yulia. She was staring sullenly out of the window. The morning sun had turned her bright red hair into a halo of fire. When I had found them, my niece looked happy. I hadn't seen her happy for so long. I can't even remember when I last saw her laughing.

As I looked at my niece, I understood that April had taken her with good intentions. If only she could have fathomed the danger she had exposed Yulia to by removing her from the compound, she would never had done it. She had no idea how dangerous a thing she had risked because she hadn't been brought into the picture. She couldn't. Not for the time being, but...

I needed a way to bring April back into the picture.

All I'd been able to think about since the previous day had been her. How I had fucked us both out of our minds, and how at the end of it all, she had flinched at my touch. That act had bruised and angered me because I couldn't understand the reason behind it.

I never had a woman do that to me before.

The sight of her packed luggage the following morning was rejection in its most brutal form. It had shot the bullet straight into my eyes. I even cut my trip short because of her. I couldn't concentrate on anything. A few times Alex gave me a funny look. Well, what the fuck did he know? He'd never had a woman grab his cock the way April did mine.

It was drastic to put my entire domestic staff out of a job, but it was the only way to bring April back. She couldn't leave yet, no way, not when I wasn't done with her.

I looked at my watch. Anytime now, I expected her to come back. If I knew anything about her, I knew she had a big heart.

I was on the phone when her feeble knock sounded on the door. I didn't respond and kept my eye on the heavy oak for a moment before turning to watch her from the surveillance monitor by my desk. She dropped her head into her hands and then tousled her hair in frustration. For a second, she put her palms on either side of her face and closed her eyes.

When she opened them, she rapped her knuckles on the door… a lot louder this time.

I waited, enthralled even by the sight of her on my tiny monitor, until my Lawyer spoke up, "Mr. Volkov?" he called. "Are you there?"

"I am," I said and looked at the monitor in amusement as she pounded the door with her fist.

I held a hand to the speaker. "Hold on," I said to my lawyer and turned towards the door. "Come in."

A few moments later, it was swung open. She'd been in my home office before so her eyes immediately went to my chair, but when she didn't see me there, she turned and found me leaning against the mantle. She opened her mouth to speak, but stopped herself when she realized I was on the phone.

I watched her, my gaze boring into hers, until she looked away.

I finished my conversation with my lawyer, returned to my chair, and took my seat. "What do you want?" I asked.

For a second, she looked as though she was going to cry. "I want to apologize. Please don't fire everyone."

I stared at her expressionlessly.

She looked pale. There were blue shadows under her eyes. "I'll take all the blame. It was my fault, they had absolutely nothing to do with it. Why punish them when it is clear that it was my fault?"

"It's the responsibility of the entire household to ensure Yulia's safety."

"She wasn't in any danger. I just thought that it would do her some good to get out of the house. She was a bit down earlier in the day."

I watched her for a few moments and then my response came, "No."

"Yuri," she called.

At the sound of my name from her mouth, I raised my head. I wanted to hear it again.

As usual, she instantly withdrew. "I beg of you, please. I cannot have the entire household's unemployment on my conscience."

"Didn't you read the terms of your employment contract? Her removal from the compound without permission was explicitly banned."

She shut her eyes. "I am so sorry. Look Yuri, if there's something I can do to make up for it, I will."

"Fine, I'll keep everyone…"

Her eyes shot wide open.

"If you return."

She looked confused. "What do you mean?"

"You know exactly what I mean. I saw Yulia laughing for the first time in almost a year and that was because of you. I want to you to carry on doing what you were, only please do not take her out of this compound again, or you could endanger her life."

Her eyes became huge. "Why is she in danger?"

"I cannot divulge that information to you at this present moment, but you must take my word for it."

She dropped her eyes. "All right, I'll return."

I didn't let her see how glad I was with my easy victory. "Good. You may return to your duties. Call Zelda and tell her the good news."

She looked up then.

Questions I needed answers to swirled through my head, but I knew better than to ask them now. "That will be all," I said and returned my attention to my computer.

"Thank you," she said, standing up.

"Be in my room tonight," was my reply. I didn't look up until I heard the sound of the door as it banged shut behind her.

I leaned back against my chair and smiled. "That's my girl."

# CHAPTER 23

## APRIL

I would stay for Yulia and the household staff.

I'd taken the easier route earlier to run away, but thanks to Yuri, the harder path was now my only option.

The rest of the household however remained wrought in confusion for the remainder of the day. No doubt, everyone would be walking on eggshells for a while whether Yuri was in sight or not.

"I just don't get it," Sandra mouthed off later that night after dinner. She was the youngest member of the housekeeping staff and my room was one of her duties. She and I were quite friendly with each other. She was English in a household full of Russians. "He fires us all and then rehires everyone back in the space of just three hours. Including you."

I glanced back and shrugged. She didn't need more information than what she already had. Deep in thought, I tuned out the rest of the chatter in the room and retrieved my mug from the cupboard. The kettle had nearly boiled. I wanted the Chrysanthemum blend at the top of the cupboard, but as I was reaching for it, I was startled by the ring of my phone. Jumping, I put a hand to my chest.

"April, are you all right?" Orlav voiced his concern. "You've been jumpy all day."

"I would be the same if I were her," Sandra piped in.

I looked at my screen and stared for a moment at the unrecognizable number. Curious, I picked it up to find out who it was.

"Hello,"

"It's almost ten," came Yuri's voice. "Where are you?"

For a moment, I was too stunned by his voice to reply, then I was filled with embarrassment at the way he was summoning me to go to his room as if I was a prostitute he hired in front of all the other staff. I was livid, but at the same time, I had made this deal with him. And a deal is a deal. "I'll be right there." My voice was cold and hard.

"Are you going somewhere?" Margot asked.

*She knew.* "Mr. Volkov," I replied calmly. "He called for some tea."

"But he only drinks black coffee," Sandra said innocently.

I could only muster a shrug and try to ignore the eight pairs of eyes on me as I retrieved the jar of dried chrysanthemum, set up a tray, and got on my way.

"He's now living on the top floor," Margot said.

"Thanks Margot, and goodnight everybody," I called as I

went out of the door. I knew they would talk about me when I left, but there was nothing I could do about it.

His room was on the top floor of the house, however when I reached the first floor stairs, I met a dead end I wondered what was going on.

I didn't want to return to the scrutiny of the others in the kitchen so setting the tray on a nearby console, I dialed his number.

"There's an elevator on the ground floor down the hallway from my office," he said. "It's the only access to my floor. Type in the code 3372 and it will lead you straight up."

I did as instructed and found the doors to the elevator opening before me. As I stepped into its glass and chrome interior, the door swished close and I was swept up.

There was only one door past the massive centerpiece of flowers by the lift. By the time I arrived at it, I was breathing too fast.

I didn't have to knock. The moment I arrived, Yuri pulled open the door. I didn't notice anything apart from his eyes. They were piecing and seemed to sear deep into parts of me that I didn't want him to reach. Clearing my throat, I opened my mouth to speak, but before any words could come out, he rasped out his instruction, "Lose the tray."

I placed it on the floor and as I straightened, his mouth was on mine. I forgot to be furious for showing me up in front of the other staff, for treating me as if I was a prostitute. My hands fisted his shirt, desperate to hold him close... or terrified of him eventually disposing of me. I couldn't tell.

I slid my hands into his hair and gave the kiss everything I had in me. Earlier that day, I had been sure that I would never lay eyes on him again, but he had fought for us. For whatever this crazy fiery desire was between us and in that moment, I appreciated him.

I tore at his buttons as my entire body began to tremble with need for him. To be completely possessed and fucked senseless the way only he knew to do. He would be the lust of my life, of this, I was certain. Nothing else or no one else would ever compare to him.

He dragged his lips from mine. "How could you leave so easily?" he rasped out.

Panting, I grabbed at his belt buckle and began to pull at the leather.

He pulled me away from him and forced me to look into his eyes. "Talk to me," he commanded.

My eyes were hazed, the blood in my veins ablaze, but what could I say to him? It would be nothing that he wanted to hear anyway, so I tugged on the tie that cinched my cotton dress at the waist and pulled it over my head. I flung the material aside and stood before him in nothing but my underwear. I saw his eyes grow dark with lust. It was all I had.

His lust for my body.

"There is no need for us to speak," I said. "I want you desperately. It's okay for it not to go beyond that." Even as the words left my mouth, I knew they weren't true. It wasn't okay for me. I wanted more. Far more, but I knew I couldn't have it. My heart was going to be broken, but I would rather have this and a broken heart than nothing.

A heavy silence so thick you could slice through it hung in the air between us as his eyes greedily feasted on my body. Then he turned around and headed towards the bed. Facing me, he began to unbutton his shirt. He stripped quietly.

I watched him, transfixed by the pure virility of his body. My clit was swollen and throbbing as he pushed his slacks down his hips to reveal his firm butt.

I was dripping wet when I went to him then. With my hands on his shoulder to support myself, I stood on tiptoes and began to trace wet, worshiping kisses down his perfectly toned back. My pussy was pulsating with need for him.

Simultaneously, I unsnapped my bra and pressed my breasts to his warm flesh.

I felt him shudder just for a moment at the contact, but he didn't turn around. He allowed me the chance to explore and soon my mouth was on his ass. I didn't know if it would be too much, but at that moment, I didn’t care. I went down on my knees, edged my head between his legs and covered his balls with my mouth.

A soft groan escaped his lips as he spread his legs further apart.

It brought a small smile of satisfaction to my heart. I didn’t have much, but this power was mine. The two sacs were heavy with lust.

I turned myself around, and inched my way upwards, using the frame of the bed as a support until I reached the root of his cock. The rock-hard shaft was so big and stiff it looked almost painful. I ran the tip of my tongue along the thick bulging veins that snaked down the satin-smooth flesh.

With my eyes locked on his, I traced adoring kisses up the entire length until I reached the mushroom head. I covered the broad tip with mouth.

He shut his eyes, and I couldn't help my smile.

He seemed untouchable, unmovable, but by just that simple act, I was able to affect such a man seemingly larger than life itself. It seemed unreal. I focused on his pleasure wanting to give more to him than he could give to me. I sucked hard and deep, taking what I could of him into my mouth and down into my throat.

"Suck me off," he urged. "We have a long night ahead of us."

I did as I was instructed, my heart brimming with excitement at the promise. I lapped up his pre-cum, and felt utterly amazed at how much I relished the taste of him. With the other few guys I had had in my lifetime, I had never bothered going this far, but with Yuri, I couldn't get enough of all that was him. To my body, this man walked on water. My mouth worshipped him. I let him do what I had never let another man do.

I let him hold my head and fuck my mouth.

When he was almost about to climax, he pulled out of me and asked me to open my mouth. He fisted his cock and pumped it hard until he began to spurt. He growled with pleasure as he watched the hot spurts of cum fill my mouth. I didn't swallow immediately. I swirled it around in my mouth and only when he told me to swallow did I obey.

I was hauled off the floor and dumped on the bed. He dived at me. My panties were rendered into shreds and my legs were thrown wide open.

My back arched off the bed as he buried his face into my soaked cunt and took my clit in his mouth.

"Unhh," I cried out helplessly, fisting the sheets. I rocked my hips with abandon, as his tongue licked me clean, until another bout of my thick arousal coated his mouth. It was a never-ending cycle of ravenous devouring. I could barely stand the intense pleasure, but I couldn't dream of being deprived of it.

"Yuri," I called out his name, my head thrashing from side to side, as his tongue plunged into me, sucking and nipping without ceremony.

*"Yuri!"*

He dug his fingers into me, and I collapsed back unto the bed.

"Oh, Yuri…"

His tongue and fingers tortured me mercilessly until I grabbed at his hair in a plea for a moment's break, but he didn't stop. "Yuri, Yuri, Yuri."

When I came, it was all over his face, shamelessly, the unending waves of mind-blowing orgasm crashing through my entire body. I shuddered on the bed, my hands clenching the sheets hard to contain the explosion of my battered clit. His head was trapped between my clenched thighs, but he didn't seem to mind as he lapped up the juices gushing out of me.

I couldn't believe our intimacy. How could we be this exposed to each other in one moment and then act like strangers in the next? I couldn't understand it. I wanted to hold him close to me, and never let go. In that moment when my brain had lost most of its function that was exactly what I did.

I pulled Yuri up and held him tightly to my breast, my arms around him in a desperate embrace. He felt like home, something I'd only ever gotten glimpses of. I wanted to kiss every inch of his body, to treasure him as mine, and no one else's even if it was just for this moment.

I was about to let him go, aware that I was beginning to cross unspoken boundaries, when he slipped his hand around me, and rolled over, until I was on top him. I kept still. I shut my eyes as he pulled me up and buried my face in his neck. For a moment I felt confused, but before I could lose the moment that I was sure would end in a snap, I cradled his head, and breathed him in, hiding my face in his neck, and matching the rise and fall of his heaving chest to mine.

And then it began again. There were condoms by the bedside. We worshiped each other's bodies for hours. Until he fell asleep, his hand cupped possessively around one of my breasts.

# CHAPTER 24

## YURI

I awoke alone, my mind coming awake instantly. Her smell lingered, but when I turned in search of her, she was gone.

I'd fallen asleep to the feel of her full breast inside my palm, the beat of her heart in my ear. Her scent, both of her hair and skin, had been of lavender. My mouth was haunted by the taste of her.

I gazed blindly at the ceiling. A strange overwhelming sensation of warmth flooded me when I thought about what she'd done. She had pulled me up to her and held me in her arms. Silently. As if we were one body. No woman had ever done that to me. No woman would have dared try.

I vaulted upright. It was dark in my room. The digital clock by my bedside showed that it was half past three in the morning. She could have waited until at least the morning to leave, but I would be willing to bet she ran off the moment I fell asleep.

I couldn't understand her. She wanted me with as much

ferocity as I did her, but almost as soon as the sex was over, she became distant. Was it fear? Did she fear me? Had I gone too far by allowing her to see that loser's corpse?

I put my feet on the ground, and realized that she was the first woman who'd been able to move without waking me. No matter how exhausted I might be, I never relaxed enough to sleep deeply when there was another body in the bed with me. She'd unraveled me and brought all my walls down with such ease that it shocked me. I on the other hand held as much impact to her as a rock...beyond our fucking sessions, that is.

Funny thing was, this is exactly the reaction I preferred from my conquests, so why did it irritate me so much when she did it? I got out of bed, seething. My body felt hot and restless.

I headed over to the bathroom. Even the thought of her had my dick rising. I forewent the piss, and just got into the shower. I let the water and the memory of her mouth as she had sucked me nearly out of my mind, wash over me. I redirected my anger into pure lust and pumped myself brutally. I saw myself grabbing her hips and fucking her so damn hard she screamed for mercy. And still I didn't stop.

My release came and it was sweet, but it left me empty. I remember the shocking way I had come at the gun range. Never before had it felt like that. In fact, I was sure I had for a little while, lost consciousness of the world around me. For hours after I was still reeling, deep in thought, and nursing a longing that was nothing short of cruel.

I switched off the water and leaned against the tiles. Alex always said life's a funny thing. It's all fun and games until someone loses a fucking eye. Yeah, I'd been fucking around all my life and now I was in danger of losing more than an eye. I pulled a towel around my hips.

Even now, I felt dissatisfied. I knew without doubt I couldn't go back to sleep. I had to finish what we begun...

The mere thought of going in and out of her pussy, relishing the clench of her tight walls on my dick, had me opening my bedroom door and making my way towards her room.

I pushed her door open, and walked in. She had turned on the AC too high, and the room was freezing cold. Certain that it would be much too cold for her, I turned it down and pulled open the draperies that hung over her windows. I cracked open a window to ensure some ventilation. The sky was starless.

The only light was from the lamps outside seeping in from the crack in the draperies. Silently, I stood and watched her, hair fanned out over the pillow, and her lush body curved into a ball.

*Maybe she just prefers sleeping alone,* a voice said in my head, and I felt my anger dissipate and in its place a totally foreign feeling of tenderness.

Dropping the towel to the floor, I climbed into bed next to her. I was desperate for her flesh, but she was so deeply asleep she didn't move even when my weight depressed the bed. I watched her for a little while more, unwilling to wake her when she so obviously needed the sleep, but my eyes slipped down to the curve of her neck and I saw the marks I'd left there. I couldn't bear it anymore. I touched the silk of her face.

She stirred and opened her eyes. She blinked, but didn't seem afraid, or even startled. Instead, her gaze moved quickly and hungrily over my body and she seemed to relish the sight of my reclined position against her headboard and my upright cock.

She lifted her arms to me in a childlike gesture and I knew then that she was still partly asleep. Her brain hadn't kicked in fully, otherwise she would have held back. As she always did.

I accepted the crush of her lips against mine. It was so innocent and so tender it knocked the breath out of me and sent the sweetest torrent of sensations racing into my veins. It crept its way to my heart. I fell back onto her bed as she rose to her knees and pulled her cotton nightgown over her head. She looked down at me. She was so beautiful it was as if I was looking at an angel, and for a second... I felt fear. It's all fun and games until someone loses an eye. How strange?

*My heart was alive!*

It hadn't beat in this way for anyone. Not from the day my father had strangled my mother right in front of my eyes because he believed she had cheated on him, betrayed him with another man.

April sat astride me, watching me, as she held my face in her hands, so softly, so delicately.

With my eyes wide open in the blue light, her body looked like porcelain, beautiful and so fragile, but then she lifted her hips and impaled herself on my cock with the brutality of an impatient lover.

A groan tore out of my throat.... my hands slid into her hair. "Go slow," I said.

Her gasp of pleasure was music to my years, soft... wrenching. This time I wanted her, slowly, deliberately. I wanted to savor all of this, until we exploded together. With all the other women, the peak had been everything. The cherry on top. With April, I wanted to savor every part of the cake.

She writhed and ground against me, slowly; her wet, greedy cunt buttering my cock with her cream. Her eyes closed her face full of ecstasy as she teased and promised me mindless bliss.

Until I couldn't take it anymore.

With a hand around her, I rolled us over and plunged my cock into her. In the dim light, I saw the love bite on her neck. Like a man in a desert who sees a well full of cool water, I moved towards it. I buried my face in her neck and sucked on that shadow, and my tongue felt the blood that raced frantically underneath.

She held me to her as though she would never let go as I began to rock her. She urged me on, eager to reach the edge, but I slowed her down, and showed her what I wanted between us.

I took her nipple between my teeth and her back arched off the bed, bringing a smile to my face. The way she responded was real and without any pretense or artifice. She didn't try to look sexy or hold back.

Our hips rose and fell with my pace, shallow then deep, rapid and then excruciatingly slow. I savored each moment in her at some point almost forcing myself to swear that it would be my last. This was nothing but pure danger that I was sinking myself into.

I told her to rest her ankles on my shoulders. She obeyed and immediately, I felt her pussy grip my cock so tightly, I cussed. My body began to shudder as we neared our peak, or perhaps it was hers, I couldn't tell, I was slowly losing coherence. The edge was beckoning, but for the first time in my life, I didn't want to go to it on my own. I wanted to take her with me.

"Come, April. Let yourself come."

She came then, beautifully with a tortuous and nearly soundless scream that she couldn't contain. Tears rolled down her cheeks as she moved her head and bit down on my shoulder.

The violence was perfect. It set me off. As I exploded inside her, the image of her tears in my mind's eyes brought such awe that I had to grip my hair. If I could cry, it would be for her and in this way too, willingly and without a single regret.

For some weird reason, I thought of my father, his dark hands around the slender stem of my mother's neck. And how she begged him, told him she needed him. I was eight years old and I learned an important lesson that night.

Don't trust anyone. Ever. Especially, if they tell you they need you.

# CHAPTER 25

## APRIL

This time it was me who fell asleep and it was him who left. I woke up to the sound of my alarm in an empty bed. He didn't appear at breakfast and the next time I caught a glimpse of him was as he walked towards his car just before lunch. His gaze slid over me for a brief second before continuing on his way, Alex strolling behind him.

Anger surged through me and before I could stop myself, I brought out my phone and called him. He didn't pick up as I pictured him getting into his car. I kept dialing, desperate, or probably out of my mind to show that I too, could be cold and flippant when I spoke to him.

Eventually, he picked up and didn't say a word leaving me to take the stage with my pitiful play. I straightened my back and launched in, "You haven't seen Yulia since yesterday."

I wanted an explanation from him, needed it, even though it was more for myself than the beautiful little girl.

He gave none, and went on to pass out his next instruction, "A new psychologist will be flying in from the U.S to examine her today." He paused. "I'll send a car to pick both of you up at three. Be ready." Then he ended the call.

I almost flung the phone into the wall.

"Bread must be left alone for it to rise. Not everything can be rushed," Zelda said softly.

Her voice broke through before I could admit to myself what was beginning to happen to me. I clenched my hands into fists and turned to her.

It was wisdom that didn't soothe me. She did not understand. I was falling in love with a man who took his pleasure then treated me as if I was a blob of gum on his shoe. Hiding my unhappiness, I went to check on Yulia and her tutor in the grand study on the second floor.

At three exactly, a sleek Range Rover came for us.

Yulia had picked out her outfit of a lace embellished denim dress. She'd complemented her outfit with a pair of brown boots and allowed me to curl her hair into soft waves. She looked heart-meltingly lovely.

"You look gorgeous," I said.

She went to the trouble of taking her notebook out and wrote:

Thank you, April. :-) So do you!

I laughed. Nothing could be further from the truth. I was dressed in a pair of jeans I owned, and a loose T-shirt. My hair was still in the bun I had piled on the top of my head earlier that morning. By now, tendrils were escaping with a vengeance. I had no makeup and but a lick of lip balm across my lips.

I wanted so badly to take a glimpse at the gigantic mirror in the foyer of the house as we passed by, for my own self-respect at least, however none of that had mattered in my nonchalant approach towards anything that had to do with Yuri, except his beautiful niece, of course.

I turned as she nudged at me in the backseat with her notepad, and I took the pink stationery from her where she had scribbled.

Where are we going?

"To see your uncle," I replied. "You haven't seen him since yesterday, have you?"

The light that had been in her eyes immediately dimmed.

To my surprise, I noted that it had been replaced by outright fear and worry. She turned away from me, and once again, I was beyond confused. I lightly touched her arm, and tried to get her attention. "Yulia," I called softly. "What's wrong?"

She didn't respond or write another word until we arrived at Canary Wharf and pulled up in front of the wonder of steel and glass that was Volkov Industries.

As I stared at the glistening skyscraper, I felt my first tiny bout of panic at my shabby appearance. For some reason, I had stupidly assumed we would be heading to a place that was similar to the construction yard where I went for my gun training.

The chauffeur pulled up and parked in front of the entrance of the building.

To my dismay, I noticed the sophisticated influx and outflow of executives in polished oxfords and shoes. My back hunched with regret. I should have worn one of my two dresses. Anything would have been better than what I was wearing. "We're at the main office?" I asked the chauffeur. He was wearing sunglasses so I couldn't see his expression, but I noted that even he was dressed with dignity in his pristine dark suit. It was with that insecure state of mind that I walked into the building with Yulia.

We were seen immediately across the expansive, seemingly endless lobby made of marble. A man wearing a pink tie, he could have been gay or just effeminate, ran up to us and introduced himself as one of Mr. Volkov's assistants. He told us his title, but it didn't register. I was too self-conscious of being the only person who looked like a hobo.

He took us past a row of flawlessly put together receptionists granting access and exit to authorized guests and herded us towards a transparent, private elevator.

A middle-aged woman guided us after we'd been delivered by the man with the pink tie on the 14th floor. She took us to a different elevator where she had to tap her fingerprint and card to open the car's doors.

Yulia and I got in.

With a kind smile, she said to us, "It will go straight to the top. Taylor will receive you there."

I wanted to ask if Taylor was male, because my battered esteem couldn't cope with some beautiful assistant who looked at me with contempt, but I kept my mouth shut and rode the elevator with a very somber Yulia. I looked down at the hand she had in mine and it felt as if with every floor we passed, her hold was getting tighter and tighter.

I gazed down as we rode upward towards the symbol of Yuri's dynasty. I could hardly believe he was the same human who had plunged into me. The one I had so daringly teased, fucked, and even *slapped!*

Now that I took this all in, it made sense why I was so easy to ignore. He was worth all of this and I was the nanny. Yes, I had a place in his life, but it was clear that looking to move even an inch out of that small space would only cause me more grief than I could handle. I'd known this instinctively, but somehow in the last two days I had allowed myself to forget.

Not anymore.

We eventually arrived at the top floor and I stepped out to the consolation that Taylor was indeed male, with a curly head of hair and a soft gaze. I pretended to myself it was because I didn't want to be looked down on by a high and mighty female employee, but the truth was I was wildly jealous. I couldn't bear the thought that he was working closely with a beautiful woman.

"Miss Winters," he greeted with a nod and a smile, before crouching down to meet my little companion. "Hello Yulia," he said with a big smile.

She stared at him with eyes that seemed haunted.

He frowned. "Yulia are you okay? What's wrong, sweetie?"

She shook her head and he turned to me.

I shrugged my shoulders. I was equally perplexed. "She's been like that since we got in the car."

"Hmm...Maybe she's dreading her session with the psychiatrist. She's been through a couple of these in a short amount of time."

"Perhaps," I responded, and just then there were voices down the hallway.

We all looked up and there was Yuri, dressed in only his shirt and navy blue suit trousers. He had loosened his tie and was strolling amidst two men dressed surprisingly casually in T-shirt and jackets. He noticed us immediately but kept his attention on the two men, their voices hushed, until they shook hands and walked away. Yuri ducked into a nearby door and the two men came towards us. As they walked past us towards the elevator, they nodded at Yulia.

The moment the doors slid shut, Yulia began to cry softy.

"Hey," I said, crouching down in front of her. She flung her arms around me and held on tightly so I lifted her up with me.

"I'll show you to the waiting lounge," Taylor said to me.

I followed, confused about what was going on.

# CHAPTER 26

## YURI

Alex was waiting for me in the office, and the moment I returned, he noted my mood. Naturally, being Alex he didn't say a word until I was seated and scrolling through the coroner's report I had just received.

"What's going on with you, huh?"

I rubbed the back of my neck. What should I tell him? April was here, so all I wanted was to bring her into this office and fuck her. "Nothing," I muttered. "Just want to get this business over with as soon as possible."

Actually, I didn't even know why I had brought her here. This space was all mine. I built this. Not my father, nor my brother had any input. I inherited the construction branch of our family business and I built this out of that corrupt money laundering shell. A job that would cost a half million would be booked at two million and everybody was happy. The banks, the contractors, the buyers, the sellers. The one who lucked out was the Tax man.

I guess if I were to be honest, I brought her here because I'd already gotten her response to the brusqueness of the yard, but this was the side that the whole world saw. Was she impressed? She sure didn't make an effort. Yeah, I surprised myself. Looks like I wasn't above trying to impress April Winters.

Her large T-shirt and messy hair had contrasted deeply with the environment, but to me she seemed perfect, a sight to awaken a blind man. I'd wanted to linger, and even move closer to speak to her. I had deliberately kept out of her way to test myself. To see if I could keep away, but who was I kidding? I had missed her like crazy this morning. It had pissed her off, that was for sure, but I was unapologetic. Much more of her and I would become an unstable fool over her.

Taylor came in. "Where should Miss Winters remain while Yulia has her session?" he asked.

I refused to meet Alex's eyes. "Bring her in here," I said and returned to my documents.

Alex rose to his feet, a quiet laughter bubbling out of his throat.

I shut my eyes, annoyed with him and myself.

"Who exactly fucked who?" he mocked.

In my current mood, I reacted badly. I flung the first thing my hand connected with at him. It was a heavy pen holder, but just as I had expected, he swerved without breaking a sweat, but it went straight for Taylor. Missing his right eye by a mere inch, it slammed into his forehead, and took the poor kid down.

I shot up in alarm. *Shit.* "Are you okay?"

With one hand, Alex pulled him up.

In spite of the blood dripping from his busted head, Taylor forced a painful smile onto his face. “I’m fine, Sir,” he said, as he limped away.

Alex shot me a cold look. With a despairing shake of his sarcastic head, he exited my office.

I collapsed down into my chair, loosened my tie even further from my neck, and ran my hand through my hair. What a fuck-up!

A short while later, Taylor returned, a bandage over his cut and carrying a tray of beverages. “Miss Winters insists on waiting downstairs in the lobby,” he said.

I lost it. “Get her the fuck in here right now!” I roared.

He hurried away from the room as quickly as he could. I pushed away the files before me on the desk and glued my eyes to the door. I knew I was acting unhinged, but I couldn’t help myself. Where April was concerned I was like a bear with a sore butt.

When it opened a short while later, Taylor knew better than to come in. April walked in and the door was shut after her. She stared directly at me without fear or caution.

“Why did you want to wait downstairs?” I asked.

She shrugged her shoulders in response.

“Answer me when I fucking talk to you,” I growled.

I watched her face darken. “Is there a good reason why you’re speaking to me like this?” she asked quietly.

I sighed, defeated before I even began. "Sit," I said, waving my hand towards the chair in front of my desk.

"Thanks but I'd rather wait downstairs."

I glared at her and she did the same. Then she turned around to walk out of my office.

I was out of the seat and across the room in long furious strides before she had a chance to even reach the doorknob.

I gripped her arm and pinned her against the door.

She was breathing heavily and for a moment, I was sure that her eyes mocked my lack of self-control at her presence. "You're very violent Yuri," she grated. "Harassing me seems to come as second nature to you."

"And you're very flippant April," I shot back. "Disrespecting me seems to come very easily to you." I was close to her now, her scent swirling around me like an aphrodisiac, intoxicating me.

Her gaze bored into mine as her chest rose and fell quickly.

It was clear. Neither of us wanted to back down.

So we met the only way we could and in the way that didn't need any reason. She reached for me with her lips and I went after her with all I had. Her unique flavor registered in my head and my entire body came alive with crazed lust. I really was like an addict. I'm not sane unless I'm fucking mating with her.

I was hard, achingly so and devoured the mouth that I'd starved myself from this morning.

Neither of us said a word but none was needed. The need,

the anger, the frustration, and the confusion about what the hell was happening to us was all evident in the way we consumed each other. In one moment, my hands were on her face to hold her in place and in the next around her waist, needing there to not even be an inch of space between us. My lips were on her neck, and in the next second, they were covering her breasts. She ground her hips into my rock hard dick and I cursed at her choice of outfit.

"Wear fucking dresses more often," I spat.

She gripped my shirt in fury forcing me to stop and look at her. "Stop telling me what to fucking do."

"I'm your damn boss," I reminded.

"Not in this damn moment," she declared.

"We'll see about that," was my response as I simultaneously yanked both her panties and jeans down her hips. I palmed her soaked pussy and she groaned into my neck. Just as I slipped two fingers inside of her, the door that connected my office to the boardroom was thrown open.

She gasped in fear and I instantly moved to cover her from view, slamming my hips against hers. It was fucking Alex. I was going to start hating him soon if he carried on like this much longer.

I turned my head, and glaring at him, and roared, "Get the fuck out."

As if he'd found me doing nothing more than sipping coffee, he headed over to the table, and retrieved his phone from it. Alex never forgot anything except on purpose. He was the most vigilant bastard I knew.

"Doctor Clover is on his way up," he threw over his shoulder in Russian as he sauntered out of the door. "Keep your voices down."

I swore to deal with him later on as he slammed the door shut. Turning back, I found April's face buried in my chest. I waited, and when she eventually found the courage to raise it up to mine, my heart melted at the sweet shade of pink her entire face had become.

"We have five mins," I said.

She looked as though she wasn't convinced that we should continue on. I took away the decision and gripped her thighs. In one smooth movement, her legs were off the floor and encircled around me. With one hand, I held her in place and with the other, I made quick work of unzipping my fly.

My cock sprung out and the moment she saw it her pupils dilated. She reached for it and for a few moments, I let her stroke it adoringly.

"How are you so fucking big?" she asked.

My eyes widened slightly. It was the first time I had heard her talk dirty to me, and I sure as hell liked it.

"How are you so fucking sweet?" I muttered.

The smile that spread across her face was deliciously erotic. There was no point fighting it. I just completely surrendered to her incontestable hold over me and I slammed into her.

She grabbed my shoulders, urging me on, and I began to pound furiously into her. This was priceless. To be able to feel like this with her.... I felt myself shudder.

We climaxed in less than five minutes.

# CHAPTER 27

## APRIL

I sensed his presence the moment he came into the kitchen.

It was past midnight, and the whole household was asleep, or so I had thought. A craving for the blend of chamomile I was slowly getting addicted to had driven me down for a midnight refreshment.

He was soundless as he approached, and my heartbeat felt as if it was disconcertingly loud in the deadly quiet room. Without a word, I went on my tiptoes to reach for the jar in the cupboard above. He came up behind me and retrieved the jar on my behalf. I froze at the contact. It was simple, but so intimate it made my chest hurt. His warmth intoxicated me as he placed the jar down on the counter and turned around without a word to leave.

He was almost at the door when I spun around and asked, "Do you want a cup of tea?" I asked. I hadn't switched on all the lights and the only lighting came from a row of lights over the fridge. It was enough to see his gorgeous eyes.

"I don't drink tea."

It was a rejection. All we ever did was fuck. He wouldn't even share a quiet drink with me. I nodded politely and quickly turned back. No problem. At least he was consistent. He didn't give me false hope.

"I'd love a coffee instead," he said.

He couldn't see me, but my lips broke into the biggest grin my muscles could stretch into. To my great delight, I heard the scrape of a chair. He was taking a seat by the table in the corner.

I didn't turn back around until his cup was ready. I took both our beverages to the table and placed his before him.

"Thanks," he murmured, and took a sip from his drink.

I did the same. I knew his eyes were on me, and it made the hairs on my body stand on end.

"How was Yulia today after her appointment with her new psychiatrist?"

"She seemed relieved. I could be wrong, but I think she is hiding something."

He frowned. "What do you mean?"

"I don't have any proof or evidence, but I got the feeling that she was terrified to meet the new psychiatrist because she was afraid the man would have some new technique that would make her reveal her secret."

He sat back. "What could she possibly be scared of or hiding?"

I shook my head. "No idea, but maybe if I can get her to trust me enough, she might tell me."

He nodded. "You've done a good job so far. Thank you."

I'd never heard him sound so sincere in his praise in all the time I had been at the house and it made me feel a warm flush of pride. "You're welcome."

"Is this yours?" he asked, indicating a book I was reading about leather working."

I nodded.

"Why are you reading it?" he asked curiously.

"It's my hobby," I replied. "I mentioned this is my resume."

"Hmm," was his response which simply meant he had glossed over it.

It was totally senseless, but I felt a sting. I was becoming too sensitive. What did I expect? That my billionaire boss would be interested in the hobbies of his niece's nanny?

"Why leather working?" He seemed genuinely interested now.

"Well, creating beautiful things makes me happy. I didn't..." I hesitated, then I just let it out, "I didn't grow up with much, so perhaps that's why I appreciate more than most, beautiful things and places. Like your home for instance. It's incredibly beautiful."

"So you're happy here?" His eyes were on me over the rim of his cup as he took another sip.

I didn't back down from his gaze. "I'm not sad."

His was a simple nod, as he drained his cup.

*Would you like another?* The question begged to be asked, but I kept my mouth shut. He would leave and I resigned myself to that fact. My heart wanted so desperately for him to ask me more, though.

He rose to his feet, and a question popped out of me, "What about you? What makes you happy?"

"I don't know what that means," he answered slowly. "I do know I'm not sad, and that's simply because I'm not dead. And neither is Alex or Yulia. That's more than I could ever ask for."

I stared at him in astonishment. He was a billionaire, he had the life most people only could dream of. He was good looking, had a great body, he had youth, and all he could be grateful for was that he, Yulia and Alex weren't dead? Jesus. Thank God, I was poor!

He rolled his head and stretched his arms. I watched his hair, a dark wavy mass brush his collar. I thought of the times I had run my hands through the silky strands. It was perfectly beautiful and so wildly sexy, but I wanted to hold him back even if it was with just one more sentence to him. His hair was the only topic of neutrality I could zero in on. My mouth opened and words tumbled out, "You need a haircut."

"What I need is to fuck you," he said flatly.

Laughter that I didn't expect bubbled out of my lips.

His mouth stretched into a full grin that made my heart swell with so much emotion I was sure it would burst. "But you were just about to leave," I pointed out.

"I'm exhausted," he confessed. "I returned barely an hour ago. It was a long day. I would probably have found my way later on to your room." He looked down at himself. "God, I'm already so fucking hard."

"Why don't I cut your hair? Then while I wash it, you can fuck me however you want. That should be a good usher into a good night's sleep for you."

"More like a restless night… My dick is fucking insatiable when it comes to you." He eyed me for a moment. "Sure you can handle it? The last female that cut my hair was shot dead."

All the amusement I'd felt, disappeared. "Why? Because she did a bad job? Please tell me you're joking."

"I'm not." He shook his head and grimaced. "But it was for a reason way less sensible than giving me a bad haircut would have been."

I was stunned to silence.

"The good news is that I didn't do the killing, so you're safe no matter how the haircut goes."

I turned away, still shaken. "You have a peculiar sense of humor."

"I know," he said. "It's sick, but it's the only way I've been able to survive." His eyes narrowed on me. "I'm going to teach you how to use a gun as you cut my hair."

I spun around, my eyes rounding.

"No discussions. It is more for my peace of mind than your safety. I will ensure that you never have the need to use one."

I couldn't refuse him when he put it in that way. I was already wading in murky waters, it made sense to protect myself as much as I could, so I was less likely to drown. So tonight, I would learn to shoot.

Yuri moved slightly and the light fell on him. He really did look tired. It was etched into his face.

My gaze softened of its own accord. "I'll be there," I whispered.

# CHAPTER 28

## YURI

I knew more than I wished I did about April, but instead of being bored, I wanted to know even more.

More than her foster background, her best friend Charlotte, and the mother who had abandoned her, but was still alive somewhere in middle Britain, I wanted to know the kinds of foods she loved to eat the most. I'd passed by a bakery with an assortment of pastries in the window as I had driven home that night, and I wondered what she loved. Did she prefer the summer or the winter? Or what other inconsequential things the rest of the world concerned themselves with that were not guns and death, did she love or hate?

There was no chair in my bathroom, so I carried one of the stools from the bedroom lounge and sat in front of the massive bathroom mirror while she faced me with a pair of scissors.

It was an intrinsic part of me to be wary whenever weapons of any sort were in my vicinity, but with April, I actually shut my eyes and allowed her to work. I listened to the sound of her quiet breathing, and reveled in her warm scent.

"Aren't you scared I'll mess up your entire head?" she teased as she snipped away.

I smiled. "If it's too bad I'll just shave it all off."

She stopped then and I opened my eyes to look at her. Hers were very green and very wide. My pulse quickened, but I ignored it. "It's just hair," I said softly. "There are worse things to deal with."

We were silent as we stared at each other, then she hastily returned her attention back to my hair.

I reached out and pulled her hips into my face.

"Hey!" she scolded, but I grabbed her full ass and nudged up her T-shirt with my nose. I kissed her stomach and she held onto my head.

Before she could move fast enough to stop me, I was on my knees, my head was between her legs, and I had a mouthful of her cunt. So the little minx had come to my bedroom commando!

Her body shuddered at the contact as she held onto my shoulders for support. "Yuri," she gasped. "I'm not done."

"You can finish later," I rasped, as I began to thoroughly lick and suck her swollen clit.

In time, the tools fell from her hands to join the smattering of nipped hair on the marble floor.

I rose and lifted her into my arms. In the shower stall, she ripped her shirt away and was back on me, unable to control herself. Her hands tugged on the band of my pants, and as they went down to the floor, so did she. She sucked my cock deep into her mouth and I held onto the wall for support.

I looked down and watched her lips feverishly worshipping the engorged head. Her pink tongue slid down my shaft, kissing and licking the burgeoning blue veins...then she took my balls in her mouth.

*Fuck,* I cursed and fought to catch my breath.

This woman consumed me. Guttural sounds emanated from the back of her throat as she mouth-fucked me. Her greed was beautiful to watch. All the blood left my brain as I came hard, hot spurts of cum shooting down her throat.

I pulled her up to me and crushed my lips to hers. I held her desperately to me as I drank her in. We were one. She tasted of me and I tasted of her. Before I knew what I was doing she was in my arms again, and we were exiting the bathroom.

"I thought we were taking a showe—"

I tossed her unto the bed.

She bounced and looked up at me with wide eyes.

"That will be afterwards," I said as I zeroed in on her. "Right now, I can only think of at least ten ways I need to have you."

She squealed with excitement as I took her nipples in my mouth and the sound sent tingles down my body.

More than an hour of mind-blowing sex later we collapsed against each other, spent and twisted. I was close to passing out from exhaustion. I'd had her in more positions than I could recall. She had her legs on my shoulders. I could smell her pussy. I was so tired my eyes were half-shut and yet her scent lured me. I turned my head and sucked at her poor swollen clit.

She moaned and whispered, "No more, Yuri. No more."

I didn't listen to her pleas.

# CHAPTER 29

## APRIL

The panic set in slowly.

Yuri was asleep and no longer available to me. The tremors of extreme sexual satiation had stopped crashing in endless waves all through my body. All I was left with was the panic of knowing there could be no turning back. From day one, I knew this unearthly attraction was dangerous. It set a fire inside of me, but I thought I could control it. But now it looked as it would grow and grow until it consumed me whole.

I wanted to run.

Attachment was what I feared most because people broke your heart. And people like Yuri, they were the worst. They had their own hell to deal with. Walls were what had kept me safe... walls were what kept me sane.

I was falling, fast and deeply for this unknowable beast of a man. It was a bad sign when I wanted to bare my entire self to him.

I needed to run.

But I didn't want to leave. In his arms, at that moment, it all felt like home. At least what I imagined home would feel like, warm and safe and full of love. But there was neither warmth, safety or love here. Tears filled my eyes. I wanted to stay, but falling asleep with him would be breaking another rule.

He was dead to the world, but I moved as quietly as I could. Try as I might, I found him impossible to budge. His thick biceps pinned me solidly to the bed. I wrenched his arm from me and he came awake.

He didn't awaken fully, but enough to ask me where I was headed.

"I need to use the bathroom," I replied.

He yawned, mumbled something, and moved away in quiet agreement.

I was freed. I grabbed my clothes, pulled open his door and sped down the hallway. Hopefully, he would assume I left just before the sun arose. Either way, it wouldn't bother him.

However, I had to protect me.

No one else would.

# CHAPTER 30

## APRIL

"You ran away?" Charlotte asked.

I spun back around to face her. We were shopping at our local supermarket. "I didn't run away," I refuted. "I just went back to my room."

"What about his hair, then?"

I smiled. "I think he must have called his own hairdresser the next morning because it looked pretty good when he met Yulia and I for breakfast."

She stared at me for a few moments and then she peered down into our cart. "Okay," she said and picked up the bag of dumplings to return back to the shelf.

"Hey!" I called.

"What? I have enough problems of my own. I don't need to point yours out."

"That's not what I meant. What I mean is…" I took a deep

breath at my inability to properly communicate. "Why are you putting the food back?"

"I don't need dumplings."

"What do you mean? You're obsessed with them."

"Well, I need a break from it."

I looked into the cart and noticed then that other items had gone missing from it. "Where are my chicken wings?"

"We already have an entire pack of drumsticks."

"I want chicken wings," I said.

She straightened to give me a dry look as though she were putting up with a toddler. "It all tastes the same."

I looked back into the cart. "Where are the baby sausages? And oh my God, the yoghurt flapjacks!"

"I don't need all of those," she said.

I searched through the cart then looked back up at her in bewilderment. "Charlotte!"

She sighed. "I'm broke okay? Until things get better, I have to scrimp and cut down on expenses."

"You're broke? What do you..." Things fell into place in flash. "Why?"

"I had an unexpected expense and I quit my job," she said.

My eyes widened. "When? Why didn't you tell me?"

"You had your own stuff to handle. It was when Yulia came over."

"What was it?"

"My boss was a bitch. Nothing I ever did was right. Why is Francine awake this early? Why is she awake this late? Don't you think that portion is too much for her? Don't you think these clothes are not flattering on her? You bought the damn freaking clothes, you freak," she yelled. She took a calming breath. "In the end, I just wanted to poison her stupid ass."

"Oh, Charlotte. I'm so sorry."

"I envy you," she said with a bitter smile. "At least yours is fucking your brains out."

"There's not much beyond that to envy. If I fall for him, I'm screwed."

"What if he falls in love with you too?" she asked.

I stopped. The thought had never even crossed my mind. Not even in my dreams did I ever imagine that possibility.

Her lips slowly stretched into a thin smile. "You didn't think of that one did you?"

"Impossible," I muttered under my breath.

"Okay," she said and pushed the cart ahead of me.

I hurried after her. "No, I'm serious Charlotte. He's a super successful billionaire. He could have anyone he wants. He would never do that. Haven't you met him? Men like that are hard and cold." I paused. "They're beyond salvation."

She stopped and turned, eyes widened with concern. "So he's dead to you?"

I was confused. "What do you mean?"

She eyed me with amusement as she grabbed a bag of potatoes and continued on her way.

The mockery eventually registered. "He's too dangerous, Charlotte."

"Okay, then get out of his house."

"I've tried, remember?"

She stopped. "So now you're his hostage? Do you want me to call the police?"

"This isn't funny Charlotte."

She gave me an apologetic smile. "I know, I'm sorry, but it's high time you let down your walls. You've had them forever. I still don't even know how I was able to find a crack in."

"I made the crack for you," I said and threw my arm around her.

She tried to displace it, but eventually just gave up and hugged me back. "Then make one also for him," she whispered in my ear.

"No," I said instantly, pulling back. "He's not asking for one, and I do not need any heartbreaks in my repertoire."

"Come on. What do you have to lose?"

*What did I have to lose?* "My sanity."

"It would be great if you lost that for once. You overthink every goddamn thing. It even took you almost a month to decide to live with me, my God."

I shifted. "Well, it was a big decision. I was afraid I could be ruining a good thing."

"And all your fears were unfounded."

I sighed. "My life is already complicated enough. I don't need to turn an affair with my boss into a horrible heartbreak."

"I don't even understand why the fact that he probably owns half of London is not a matter for consideration," she said beneath her breath.

I heard her, but wanted her to repeat it. "What was that?"

Her voice went up a couple of notches. "Nothing."

"Gold digger,'" I spat.

"Self-righteous idiot," she threw back.

I tugged at her hair. "Enough about Yuri. You said you had an unexpected expense? What is it?"

She was silent for a while and then she said quietly. "My mother needed some money."

"Oh, Charlotte."

"It's okay. She's all right now. Sometimes, it's hard for her to manage on her measly pension, you know. If something breaks down, it's the end of the world."

"Listen, do you need some money?"

"Nah, I've already got another job." She crinkled her nose. "It's out in Wales though."

"Wales!" I wailed.

"It's only three hours by train." She grinned.

"Right."

"I'll be taking care of a little boy. I spoke to his mother and I really hope I'm not exchanging one bitch for another, but I've got to give it a shot. I'm desperate."

"Why can't I give you some to tide you over first?"

"No, April. I can do this on my own. I can't pull out the despair card yet. I'll be proud of myself if I get through this on my own."

"You're crazy, you know."

"I know," she said. "Will you come visit me in Wales? I think I'm going to be living in some kind of castle."

"Oh, you know, I'm scared of ghosts."

She sucked in her breath. "You just said that to put me off, didn't you?"

I began to laugh and she joined me too.

"If you played your cards right you could have your billionaire buy you a castle without ghos—"

"Stop freaking going there."

She put her hands up in defeat. "I get it. You can't stand to owe anyone and all that. Understood. But you do owe me for sticking by your side all these years, so get me Domino's tonight."

"You were the one who refused to leave me the hell alone. Why do you want pizza? What of all this food?"

"Are you going to cook? I'm freaking exhausted."

"Fine," I said.

"Order it now, so it gets home as soon as we arrive."

"Yes ma'am." I pulled my phone out of my pocket. However, just as I began to search for the number, a call from Margot came in.

"April?"

"Margot," I answered, instantly concerned. "Is everything all right?"

"Everything's fine, but Mr. Volkov just sent an order. He'll be returning from Venice today, and wants you to accompany him to an event."

For the first few seconds, I couldn't think. "An event?"

"I wasn't given the details. He's sent over some outfits for you to choose from, and says you should be ready for seven."

I took a deep breath. "All right, I'll be back in an hour." I ended the call.

Charlotte was leaning against the cart staring at me. "Why is your face like that?"

My heart was pounding in my chest. "Yuri just requested I join him for an event tonight."

She took a minute to think about it. "Isn't this a good thing?"

"He left early yesterday and made no mention of this whatsoever."

"Well... I really don't know what to say. Maybe he really missed you."

"He could have called me himself to speak to me. Since he left, he hasn't even called to ask after Yulia."

"I am officially confused by the both of you," she said. "Either way, attend the event with him."

I opened my mouth to say something.

She held up her hand. "Don't interrupt me. Attend the event and let's see what comes out of it."

"Why should I? It's not part of my job description."

"And fucking him is?" She sighed. "Whatever this event is it must be high profile, which means that he isn't reluctant to have you seen with him. That's amazing to me. He's not some random business owner, he is a billionaire. Think, April. He could have called any woman and he didn't."

"Charlotte..."

"Give this a chance. Let's figure out what he is up to. I still want that pizza though."

I called up the Dominos and ordered their biggest pizza with extra toppings and a whole pile of sides for her.

# CHAPTER 31

## APRIL

Four exquisite dresses were laid out on my bed for me.

A hot pink, figure-hugging Versace with a plunging neckline, an Olive green loose and short Christian Dior, a stark white, structured Carolina Herrera number, and a two piece, Chanel champagne train skirt with a stark white lacy bodice.

I studied them, still confused about what exactly was going on. I heard movement behind me and turned to see Zelda walk in with Sandra. They laid four pairs of shoes at the foot of the bed before straightening up to meet my bewildered gaze.

I felt strangely guilty and ashamed.

Didn't Yuri know that by doing this he was exposing our relationship, or whatever we had to the world, especially my colleagues?

The look on Sandra's face for instance was toxic. She'd been my friend and now she glared at me as if I were her enemy.

"You have an hour to turn yourself into a Princess," Zelda said, with a warm smile.

Her friendly attitude allowed me to breathe just a little bit easier.

Then Sandra chirped in, her tongue ready to do damage, "I think it now makes sense why he fired the entire house when you left, then rehired everyone when you returned. It had nothing to do with Yulia, did it?"

Zelda ignored her. "Do you need help with your hair and makeup? There is an excellent service that he suggested and—"

"It's fine Zelda," I said to her. "I'm not going. I don't really understand why he's asking me to go with him."

Sandra snorted in disgust. "Snake," she muttered under her breath, and made her way out of the room.

I was fuming as I watched her go.

Zelda gently touched my hand. "Don't pay any attention to her, she's just jealous."

"There's nothing to be jealous about," I responded, almost sorry for myself.

She gave me a reassuring pat on my arm before leaving the room.

Immediately, I picked up the phone and called Yuri. He didn't pick up. After three more tries he eventually did, and my tone was icy, "I'm not going," I declared.

Silence. "Then who's going to take care of Yulia?"

Ah, the humiliation…I retraced my steps. "What? Yulia is going to be there too?"

"Why wouldn't she be?"

I was silent and confused, both at myself and him. Before I could say another word, he ended the call. I slapped my palm to my head. Why didn't Zelda tell me? Ugh. I hurried out to find Zelda to ask about Yulia's whereabouts

"She hasn't yet returned from her session with her psychiatrist," she said with a frown.

"But Mr. Volkov said that she will be accompanying us to the event."

Zelda cocked her head in surprise. "Of that I am not aware, but maybe he has his own plans." She gazed nervously at my unchanged outfit of khaki shorts and a white tee. "Please get ready," she pleaded. "Mr. Volkov will not be pleased if you are late. I will sort Yulia out and make sure she is ready at seven."

## CHAPTER 32

### YURI

For the first few minutes after the call, nothing was said.

Then Alex spoke, "April is going to be there?

We were riding in the back of my Bentley, and on our way to the airport in Paris to catch my plane back to London. I couldn't say a word, and Alex looked away.

"I told you to fuck her, not completely lose your head to her."

He was right. I had lost my mind.

He shook his head. "I have never seen you this crazy for a woman. Why the hell do you want her out there so badly anyway? She belongs in your bed, nowhere else. You want to put a hit out on her? Don't you know the battles we're currently in the midst of right now?"

*I want to give her the chance to meet her mother,* was what came to mind. However, I didn't say it out loud. Then I would have to admit that not only had I gone out of my way to uncover it, but to ensure that her mother would be attending the event tonight.

Perhaps she didn't know the woman, in which case no harm would be done since she wouldn't even be able to recognize her, but if she did, what happened from then on would be up to her. But now with Alex's cold but completely rational rebuke, I was starting to wonder if I should have waited. Until it was safer.

But fuck it all. Why should I wait? I wanted to see her, to touch her, to have her by my side. I looked at Alex. "Don't fucking talk to me like that," I spat.

He chuckled. "You only pull out the authority card when you know you've messed up. That's good then. Screw your damn head back on. Stop letting that girl turn you into a pussy." He got out of the car before I could swing my fist in his direction, and strolled across the tarmac towards the waiting Bombardier Global 7000.

With a sigh, I did the same, and soon we were in the air.

I changed on the plane so as soon as we arrived in London I was driven straight to the Grosvenor House hotel. I stepped out to the flashing of cameras and a bright red carpet welcome. It was the annual Fulfilling Dreams charity ball hosted by the Mayor of London's office. It was in my best interest to be here and to splash the occasion with as much money as I could throw at whatever nonsensical plans they had brewing. Tonight would be nothing less than two million.

A beautiful usher met me with a dazzling smile and offered to lead me to my table.

I had other plans. "Await my plus one instead," I told her. "April Winters. Make sure to show her straight to her seat and alert me on her arrival."

My order was taken, and I turned around to the approach of the smiling face of affluent real Estate Mogul, Akshay Khan.

# CHAPTER 33

## APRIL

I *have no business being here.*

I stood in a brightly lit hallway. True, I was no less lavishly decorated in my stunning Chanel dress than anyone else in the place, but they all seemed to know what they were doing and where they were going.

The men, with gorgeous diamond-embellished women on their arms gilded by, while I stood alone, wondering what I'd gotten myself into.

I took two deep breaths...and felt even worse so I was about to leave, when I saw her.

I froze.

My mother was here. She had a man and an elegantly dressed young woman with her... and they were coming towards me. Our eyes didn't meet as they went by. I was still in shock, so I subtly started to follow them. They joined a cluster of dignitaries who they smiled and shook hands with.

"Can I help you?" someone asked.

I jumped and turned around.

An impeccably dressed usher in a dazzling sequined gown met my eyes. “Do you have your invitation card, Madam?”

“Uh, no.”

“Perhaps you are meeting someone?” Her eyebrows rose and her voice sounded a tad colder.

“Yes. I’m meeting Mr. Yuri Volkov.”

She glanced down at a clipboard she was holding. When she raised her head, she was all smiles again. “You must be April Winters?"

“I am."

She smiled. “I'll show you to your table.”

I followed, and was led to a table meant for eight. It was elegantly set with bouquets of blood red roses, and tall candles. My mind was in turmoil. I couldn’t believe she was here. What were the chances?

I told myself to hold my head up and enjoy the night no matter what happened and accepted a champagne flute from a tray carried by a passing waitress.

I settled in and with my eyes, I sought out my mother. I found her easily. I didn’t feel any emotion as I watched her smile and talk to people. A few minutes passed, then I realized that she was my mother in name only. I wanted nothing from her. Not even recognition. If nothing else, this night showed me that I could close that door once and for all. I drained my drink. I would give Yuri a few more minutes and then I would take my leave.

Music was playing, and some people were already smoothly heading to the dance floor. I watched and out of nowhere, I heard his name being called out.

"Mr. Volkov."

I turned and watched as the young woman I'd spotted with my mother ran towards him.

He stopped but his eyes were on me, and only when she reached him did he turn to her.

She flushed, and almost couldn't say a word.

Oh yes, I understood exactly what had come over her. I grabbed another drink, but it felt like shards going into my system as the liquid went down. I wanted to rise, to leave, but I couldn't move. I couldn't take my eyes off Yuri and the woman. She was laughing up at him. The table I was sitting at began to fill up. I received polite nods from the guests as they took their seats and I prayed that no one would ask me who I was.

The prayer wasn't answered.

I soon realized both the Mayor and the Deputy Prime Minister respectively were just a few seats from me. I drained the glass and wondered who the hell had seated me here.

"Hello, are you here with Yuri?" the mayor's wife asked me.

*Yes, that's right I'm a nobody. My only worth is I'm sleeping with Yuri Volkov,* I wanted to say but instead I rose to my feet. "I need to use the Ladies. Please excuse me."

I was out of there and it took everything I had not to run across the room. I kept my chin up and finally got my escape.

When I got to the restrooms, there were too many people at the mirror, so I found an empty stall, sat on it, and called Charlotte.

She didn't pick up, and I wanted to flush the phone down the toilet. I wanted her to tell me not to be cowardly, or to talk some sense into me to realize my place and to get out of here. I had no clue of what to do.

Eventually, when the bathroom quieted down, I got out of the stall and stood in front of the gigantic mirror to kill more time by reapplying my lipstick.

*Ask him about Yulia,* I reminded myself. *If she's not here then it means he tricked you. You can then leave.*

A woman came up to the mirror. I tucked my hair behind my ears. Our eyes met in the mirror and I froze.

## CHAPTER 34

APRIL

It was *my mother... a*nd she was smiling at me. My chin trembled, but somehow I was able to stretch my lips into a thin smile.

Her smile widened as she extracted a gold lipstick case from her purse.

I stared at her in amazement.

Her eyes were bright and her short hair was a beautiful dark blonde. She looked nothing at all like me, but damn she was beautiful.

"You're sitting beside Yuri Volkov," she noted.

I nodded politely in response.

"Are you two..." She raised her brow suggestively.

The smile left my face. The disappointment I felt was so great I was sure she would never be able to comprehend it. I couldn't hold back. "It's none of your business," I said tightly.

The smile left her face also.

I pretended to adjust my hair until she moved a step closer to me. I turned and looked at her.

"I don't know who you are," she said, "but you look, quite out of place here. Just because you wear a designer dress, doesn't mean you can fit into a strata of society you don't belong to. So I'm here to give you a piece of advice. Take it in the vein it is given. I'm being cruel to be kind. You are wasting your time with Yuri Volkov. He will play with you and then he will leave you for someone from his social circle." She smiled then and turned to take her leave.

"Don't you recognize me, mother?" I asked when she had already flounced away and shut the door behind her.

The tears fell from my eyes before I could stop them. "Ah, fuck," I cursed, and quickly wiped them off my face. I wouldn't let myself cry. I turned towards the mirror. My eyes were bright with unshed tears. Not here. Not among these cruel people who understood only money, power and social class.

I thought of my mother. How she had climbed the ladder herself and yet, she had tried to stop another who she recognized as a social climber. It was heartbreaking, but I understood exactly what had happened. My own mother saw me as the interloper. She was saving Yuri for that elegant young woman she had come with.

I watched myself in the mirror. What was it about me that gave me away? My hairstyle? My lack of social graces? I'm not covered in pearls and diamonds? Or something else intangible only they understood.

I straightened my shoulders. Well, they were welcome to their stupid world. I wanted nothing to do with it. I was done with this party. I would just call a taxi and go back to my own little apartment. And Yuri? He can go *fuck* himself.

I was walking out of the Ladies when my phone rang. It was Charlotte, so I picked up immediately. There was noise all around her.

"I'm really busy right now, are you okay?" she asked.

Just hearing her voice suddenly loosened the knot in my chest, and suddenly I couldn't hold the tears in anymore. They came rushing down my face. "Where are you?" I blubbered.

"I took a waitressing gig just for one night. It'll help pay some bills."

"I'm so sorry," I apologized, "I have no idea what the hell is wrong with me."

"I'm going towards the bathroom," she said "Tell me everything."

"No." I shook my head. "You might get in trouble."

"I'm in a corner now," she said to me. "You have five minutes, start talking."

With a sigh, I turned away from the main room and headed towards a quiet corridor which ended with a fire escape door. "I don't know what's wrong with me, Charlotte." I sniffed. "You know I don't normally care what people... you know, I don't let people move me. You know this, right? But I'm here. I don't have jewelry, and my...my mom's here—"

"What?" she bellowed in my ear.

"Yeah, she's here. She didn't recognize me and I didn't tell her who I was. She's with a man and a young woman. The woman knows Yuri. I think she's kind of—um... oh, God—I think she wants him, Charlotte." A sob escaped my mouth. "Oh, God, I feel so insane right now."

"Hey, calm down. You're not insane and they're not just people," she said quietly, "One is a man you just might have fallen in love with, and the other is a mom that didn't even bother to at least know what you look like. I would be thrashing out that entire gala by now if I were you. And you know me, I'm a basket case. I'm not kidding."

I almost laughed as I wiped the tears from my face with back of my hand. "I know."

"You're actually sobbing," she said in wonder. "The last time was when Bambi's mother died."

I took deep breaths. "Actually, I've cried a lot since I met that bastard."

"Whoa. How is this his fault?"

"I don't know. He just left me there."

"Give him a break. He just got back from wherever he went to."

"He was flirting with that woman."

"I thought you said she was flirting with him."

"Yeah, she looked like she wanted him to fuck her right there in front of everybody," I cried, jealousy burning in my stomach.

"So what? Even I want to climb that hard body. It doesn't

mean anything. The question is, does he want her? And if he doesn't, you have nothing to worry about."

"Well, he didn't look very encouraging…"

"Are you going to leave?"

I sighed heavily. "I think I should, don't you?"

She sucked in her breath.

"Charlotte…" I warned. It was a bad sign when she sucked in her breath.

"You're at Grosvenor House Hotel, right?"

"Yeah," I confirmed cautiously.

"Guess what? I am two minutes away. Literally next door."

"No, don't come here," I protested

"Oh fuck," she swore suddenly.

"What?"

"Almost the whole restaurant has just seen me crouching in the corner like a thief with a phone to my ear." I heard the sound of shuffling and her saying, "I'm sorry everyone. I have an idiot for a sister. You know how it is. Boyfriend problems."

"Stop... Charlotte... you won't be able to get in, anyway. They ask for your invite as soon as you get into the hallway."

"I'll get in through the back door. Waitresses in full uniform have privileges."

We laughed like two crazy girls and then she hung up.

## CHAPTER 35

### APRIL

I loitered around the Ladies. I was sure she wouldn't be able to get in, but less than five minutes later she was walking up to me in her black and white waitress uniform.

She pulled off her favorite pair of earrings from her lobes-bees carved in pearls and reached up to place them on my ears. "You said you had no jewelry. Now you do. Yeah, they're cheap and they can't be compared to the overpriced dress, or shoes you're wearing, but nobody will really know they're not real."

"Oh Charlotte, I can't wear them. I'd be too afraid of losing them. Your Dad bought these for you before he passed away."

"They are priceless to me, but so are you. That woman, who bore you, is probably the poorest creature on earth because she has no clue who she chose to forget about. You're the rarest treasure in this shallow place, April...so enjoy the rest of your dinner, and don't you dare feel less in any way than all these sad, misguided people hiding behind their designer clothes."

She brought out my hair to cover the earrings, but I tucked my hair back behind my ears and looked into her beautiful blue eyes. "They can't be hidden."

"Just try to make it through the night without losing your temper and beating someone up," she said with a smile.

"Hey, this is me you're talking to. I don't beat people up. I leave that to you."

A waiter passed by with a tray of canapes. She lifted one and put it into her mouth. "The truffles are amazing," she said. "And there's bound to be caviar coming later on. It tastes like shit but make sure to have some for the stories later on." She grinned at me. "Okay. My work here is done. I gotta go. I still need to get paid for tonight. I'm not working for nothing. Love ya." With a wave, she turned and disappeared down the hallway.

Seeing Charlotte changed everything. I got my strength. I didn't feel small or inadequate anymore. I felt strong. It was Charlotte I wanted to emulate, not these shallow people.

I returned to my table, head held high, and saw Yuri. He was already seated, but his eyes were roving the place. I knew he was looking for me.

The MC announced the Prime Minister's arrival at that moment, but I couldn't take my eyes off the man who had turned my life upside down. Dashing was a pitiful word.

Dressed in a black tuxedo, his hair was brushed back away from his face in thick effortless waves. Under the bright lights of the room, his skin was like burnished gold. I noticed the ever present and tiny furrow between his brows, but you could only see them by staring too much at him. He was so beautiful. So mysterious. So unreachable. I almost couldn't believe he had been inside me.

He stood out in the room, unmistakable, incomparable, intimidating...

From afar, he was Mr. Volkov, billionaire extraordinaire. However, to me, he somehow became Yuri, the ravishing brute that seemed to have been created not only to blow my mind but to jumble up my emotional state.

I ran my gaze down his clothes. Underneath was the sculptured chest I had trailed kisses down countless of times, and thick biceps built with raw primal strength I had dug my nails into. My gaze went back up to my second favorite place on his body. No prizes for guessing what was first on the list. Those lips. I had kissed them feverishly and they had in turn returned the favor on me—everywhere.

I slipped into my seat and smiled politely at the others at our table, but I was so aware of the man beside me I feared that I would jump if he were to even touch me. I wanted to look into his eyes to again see that primal lust which set me ablaze. Was it still there? I took the champagne flute on the table and gulped down the golden liquid until I nearly choked. I covered my mouth as a small cough escaped me. Yuri leaned into me, his body heat automatically frying my brain.

"Are you okay?" he asked.

I couldn't respond. Just gave a nod.

An orchestra performance started to play. It was a full philharmonic orchestra of not less than 60 members. I listened and allowed the heavenly sounds to soothe away my nerves.

It worked, so by the time they were finished, my applause was heartfelt.

The night wore on with speeches, most of which I couldn't fully decipher but it was all for some good or the other, so I applauded in the appropriate place. Food arrived and I played with it until expressionless waiters came to clear my plate.

Eventually, it was time to dance. Both Yuri and I stayed in our seats. People came to speak to him, but he seemed to cut off conversations quickly.

When I couldn't stand it any longer, I turned to him. "Where's Yulia?"

His response was simple, "She's not here."

"You told me that she would be," I said.

"I'm allowed to change my mind."

"She was never supposed to come, was she?"

He looked deep into my eyes. "No."

We both went quiet. Just then, someone came up to me and when I looked up, I saw that it was the young woman who'd come in with my mother. I didn't know who she was. Maybe she was my sister? I felt sad suddenly. She didn't even know she was my sister, but even worse, if she did, she would have been horrified to have a nanny for a sister.

"Could I whisper something in your ear?" she asked, her smile bright.

I nodded.

"My mother said that she already spoke to you in the bathroom and you understood. I would like to sit beside Yuri."

It took a moment for it to sink in. And it was unbearably painful. My mother knew who I was. She had recognized me. Otherwise, she would never have dared to ask me to give up the opportunity of a lifetime for a stranger.

I turned towards Yuri. I opened my mouth to ask and then closed it. This is what my mother wanted. I rose to my feet, and with a smile handed my seat over.

It was time to leave either way. I walked away from Yuri and did not look back.

## CHAPTER 36

### APRIL

The glass stem shattered between my fingers… and it startled everyone at the table.

"Mr. Volkov, are you all right?" April's half-sister asked, her eyes wide with concern.

She was beautiful, of course, but there was not one thing about her that attracted me to her. I rose to my feet.

April's mother appeared suddenly. "Mr. Volkov," she said sweetly.

A quiet explosion went off in my brain. I held her gaze and spoke very calmly, doing all I could to hold myself back, "You have two daughters, Madam. It is a shame you do not chose to recognize that, but if you do not get out of my way in five seconds, I will make sure the banks that hold all your debts recall their loans. You will lose *everything.*"

It took a second for the threat to sink in, another to realize I meant every word, and a third to convince herself I was more than capable of accomplishing exactly what I had threatened. “Get up!” she shouted in a panic to her clueless daughter. “Get the hell up.”

Barely able to contain my disgust at the ugliness of human beings, I went after April. I reached her just as she had hailed a cab. She already had the door open, but before she could get into it, I caught her arm and pulled her towards me.

She slammed into my body. “Let go of me,” she yelled and put up a fight, but she was no match for me. I waved the driver off and I dragged her to the back of my waiting Bentley. As I pulled the door open, she stopped to glare at me.

"Get in," I grated.

She refused to move.

“I seem to be the only one that you have no problems defying.”

She got into the car then, and I slid in after her. Neither of us said a word as the car sped into the night. I drew my bow tie from my neck and flung it aside.

Eventually, she spoke. “Please let me off somewhere so I can take a cab home.” When I didn’t respond, she turned to me. “Yuri.”

I was still furious. “Your home is my house,” I grated.

My driver sped all the way home and the moment we arrived, she jumped out of the car and started running at breakneck speed towards the house.

I got out and went after her.

She headed straight to her room, retrieved her luggage from the closet, and began to throw her things into it.

I grabbed the bag from the bed and flung it so hard it crashed into a free-standing mirror and shattered it to pieces.

She gazed at the chaos in shock, her eyes nearly popping out of their sockets.

"Am I a joke to you?" I snarled.

"What the hell are you talking about?"

"Why are you packing your things?"

"Because I want to leave."

"Why do you want leave?"

"I would have thought it was obvious."

I slammed the door shut behind me, and fought to control my breathing. "Answer me!" I roared

Suddenly, tears filled her eyes. "What do you want from me?"

"Let me rephrase my question. Why don't you want anything from me?"

She stared at me hopelessly. "What can you give me?" she asked. "Besides a broken heart?"

Silence.

"I thought so," she taunted. "What do you want to hear, Yuri? Or what do you want to see? You want to see me crazy in love with you? Worshipping the very ground you walk on, or crazed with jealousy, like tonight, when that bitch fearlessly came to ask for the seat beside you?"

They shared the same mother. I wondered if she realized it. "And you got up," I reminded her bitterly. "So easily."

"I have no place in your life Yuri. Isn't that what you would prefer? A fuck toy? Hmmm?"

"A fuck toy. That's rich. I invited you to accompany me and you treat me like I am nothing," I bellowed. I couldn't believe that these words were coming out of my mouth. "You gave me up to a stranger without a thought. Where did your insurmountable pride go?"

"It disappears," she said. "When people ask me for things that don't matter."

"Or yeah? And when it comes to falling asleep in my arms? Can't do that can you? Is it because it matters?"

She took a step back. "What if I fall in love with you?"

I glared at her. "I want you to be in love with me."

She looked stunned. "What?"

"Yes, I want you to fall in love with me."

"For what? So your ego can feel good about another conquest?" she demanded aggressively.

"No, because I want to take care of you."

"I don't need you to take care of me."

Silence.

"I need you by my side."

"For how long?" she spat. "Until you get tired and need another?"

I took a step towards her.

She took three steps backwards. "Don't come close to me. I need you to let me go, right now. Before it's too late."

"Before it's too late for whom?"

"I've never assumed or expected love in my life, because even the people who should be biologically programmed to give that to me, couldn't. I'm not asking you for anything, just let me go, okay?"

"Will you able to leave?" I asked her. "And forget everything about me? About us?"

"Time and my brain. They've allowed me to survive my fate thus far. I'll keep leaning on them." She started to leave.

I stopped her before she could get past the door. "Come with me to my Chateau in France. Both you and Yulia. I don't have the confidence to love you. In my world, a billion things are always on the edge of going wrong. Having you in my heart will drive me insane, but my body needs you now, and I just can't let you go. Not yet." I pulled my phone out of my pocket and made a quick call in Russian. In seconds, two hefty guards appeared at her door.

She gazed at them in disbelief.

"We will return from the chateau in a week. After that, you're free to do whatever you want."

"Are you imprisoning me?" she asked in disbelief.

"I'm making a decision for the both of us. Let's *fuck* each other out of our systems before the week is over. This madness has to burn itself out. It can't last. Nothing that burns this bright can last."

She snorted in bitter amusement. “Do you actually believe that it will work?”

“It doesn't matter if it does or not. We will be done with each other when we return from France. Not a day earlier. We’ll leave tomorrow night.”

# CHAPTER 37

## APRIL

I awoke to the sound of Yulia's laughter.

It was filled with such joy that it pulled me out of bed.

My feet landed on the floor, as the events of the previous night came to me. From the incredible fiasco with my mother and to my conversation with Yuri thereafter, it all felt unreal. It was as if I was peering through a looking glass at someone else's life.

Pulling on a pair of jeans, I headed over to the window where the sound was coming from. She was indeed having a swell time, but with someone I didn't recognize.

He had a sparse head of thinning white hair and was pushing her on the swings, as high as she could possibly go. It made me nervous, so I hurried downstairs and out to the garden behind the house.

She squealed even louder when she saw me, and urged for the swing to come to a stop, so she could come over to give me a hug. Runnng over to me she grabbed my hand and looked up into my eyes.

I brushed her hair away from her face. She was still in her nightwear. "You haven't had a bath." I pinched lightly at her nose. "I must have overslept."

She looked slightly guilty.

I figured she must have come to my room, saw me still asleep, and tiptoed back out. I smiled at the lovely child and lifted my head to the stranger she seemed so comfortable with.

"I'm Ivan Volkov," he said, his eyes a chilling blue just like Yuri's despite the wide smile on his face. "You must be the new nanny that my niece is so in love with."

I blushed with pleasure and accepted the hand he offered. I wondered if he could be one of Yuri's older brothers, but the lines around his eyes and the grey at his temples aged him too much for that. He seemed to be in his late sixties.

"I'm her grand uncle," he explained.

I nodded. "It's a pleasure to meet you."

"I've been away in the US handling the family business, so I haven't been able to see Yulia for almost two months. I've missed her so much."

The smile that Yulia flashed up at him was open and trusting. A marked contrast to the way she treated Yuri.

"Will she be able to have breakfast with me before I have to leave?"

"There is absolutely no reason why not," I replied with a big smile. I liked him. He was polite and more importantly, he was the first person Yulia seemed to adore. "I'll quickly wash her up and we'll be down in a bit.

Half an hour later, we were all seated in the dining room with Ivan right by Yulia's side and constantly offering up bits of his food to her. He had asked for fried tomatoes and she usually never had those, but because he had ordered them, she decided she wanted some too. He gave her bites and nibbles from his fork to her absolute delight.

I watched them and wondered why she was never this way when Yuri was around.

As if on cue, all the hair at the back of my neck stood, and I knew that he must be approaching. When I looked up to his face, I had the answer to my question. His presence wasn't cold, at least to me, but he was just intimidating. Very. Unlike his uncle who just seemed like a gentle, kind, caring man.

At the entrance to the breakfast room he stopped. His face was cold and closed. He said something to his uncle in Russian and turned away to take his leave.

With a smile at Yulia, Ivan rose to his feet. He spoke to her in Russian and she nodded happily. I guess he must have promised he'd be right back.

I always poured the coffee for Yuri. It was always the first thing he consumed before he ate. "What do you think, Yulia? Shall I take some coffee in for your uncle?

She nodded.

I poured the coffee and carried it out to his study. I had just placed my knuckles on the heavy oak door to knock on it when I heard crashing sounds from within the room.

My heart jumped in my chest, as I staggered, the hot dark roast spilling all over my hands. I dropped the cup and it shattered into pieces on the granite floor. "Shit," I cursed and instantly bent down and began to pick it up.

At that moment the door was pulled open and I looked up to see Ivan standing in the doorway. To my shock he was swaying unsteadily, his face was pale, and his lip was busted.

"Are you okay?" he asked me, even though he was the one who was bleeding.

In my peripheral vision, I could see Yuri taking his seat calmly. It confused me so much that my hand tightened on a shard of porcelain cutting my finger. A soft cry escaped my lips.

Instantly, Yuri pushed out of his chair and started striding towards me.

However, Ivan was already crouching down to help me.

"April," Yuri called urgently. He looked anxious.

"It's okay. I'm fine," I replied and rose up.

"Show me," he ordered, with a frown.

"It's nothing. It's just a little cut," I said, aware of Ivan watching me. I didn't want him to know that Yuri and I were lovers.

"I'll get one of the maids to clean it up," I said and hurried away.

As I went, I heard Ivan roar out something in anger. I turned around to see that three of his security had appeared out of nowhere. They handled Ivan with less grace than should have been given to a grand uncle and in shock, I turned to gaze at Yuri.

He was watching me without any expression at all.

*This is one of the reasons we can't be together. Your world is terrifying.*

# CHAPTER 38

## APRIL

https://www.youtube.com/watch?v=Q3Kvu6Kgp88
(I Regret Nothing)

Later that night, both Yulia and I were packed, awaiting our ride to the airport. Soon an entourage of a Mercedes Benz backed by two SUVs arrived and the both of us were ushered into the Benz by Alex.

Yuri drove us personally, while the other two vehicles escorted us and in no time, we were at the airport. The door was pulled open by Brain. Waiting on the tarmac was a private plane, two air hostesses, and a pilot.

I saw another side of Alex then. Despite his enormous size, he jumped out of the car and kept an eagle eye on our transfer from the cars to the plane. Through the doorway, I could see two more security men present. It made me wonder why Yuri always had to have so much security around him. Was this all for Yulia's benefit? He did seem to be paranoid about her safety. Perhaps for the rich, the risk of being kidnapped was always foremost in their minds.

We were welcomed aboard and ushered to our seats by a pristinely polished hostess with a flawless bun, and dark red lipstick.

Yuri quickly settled himself with a laptop across his desk and started speaking in French to someone on his phone.

Yulia sat next to me while Yuri continued on with his call, his gaze alternating between her and me.

The service was excellent. We had sliced fresh fruit, finger sandwiches, little cakes and scones.

I noticed Yuri didn't eat. He worked steadily for a while before he rose to his feet and took his leave from the cabin.

When Yulia fell asleep, I carefully covered her sleeping form with a blanket and went in search of him. The plane was big, I couldn't find him so eventually, I asked Brain.

He pointed to a door. "He is in there."

I hesitated, then I reminded myself, I had absolutely nothing to fear, but the limited time I had left with him. I walked over to the door. Without knocking, I pushed it open and went in.

He was asleep, but came awake the moment I opened the door. It was a short flight so I didn't expect him to sleep, but as I gazed into his eyes, I saw how exhausted he looked.

He had undone the top button of his white shirt and had obviously just plopped himself on the top of the duvet. He looked so sexy, but as usual painfully alone.

I stopped at the foot of the bed.

"What is it?" he asked, sitting up.

I wanted to run my fingers through his sleep tousled hair, but he beat me to it.

"Yulia," I began. "Why don't you ever spend time with her?"

He sighed. "Haven't you noticed how terrified she is of me?"

"Even so. Maybe if you tried just a little bit more..."

"If I come too close to her, and show her even the slightest intention to stay, she looks like she is about to burst into tears."

"Why?" I asked. "Has your relationship with her always been this way?

"Of course not," he said, a slight tilt of his lips at a memory. "We used to be buddies, especially in her third and fifth year. But ever since I took over custodianship of her and brought her home to London with me, she has slowly withdrawn." He narrowed his gaze as he thought a bit more deeply. "No," he concluded thoughtfully. "It's a bit more recent than that. It really began at the same time she stopped speaking."

"But—"

"No more of that now," he said. "We'll talk about it more when we arrive. Right now, we only have a short time before we land."

"Oh," I said thinking he was dismissing me. I went to turn around, but he reached out and catching my hand and pulled. I fell on top of him.

The breath was knocked out of me as my chest connected with his rock hard one. Suddenly, his beautiful face was much too close. My brain stopped functioning. "Yuri," I whispered, as he brushed his thumb in slow feather like circles on the pulse in my wrist.

"Your heart is racing," he mocked.

We had one week…

A surge of emotion that I couldn't understand rushed into me at this thought, and before he could see it in my eyes, I crushed my mouth to his. The kiss was fervent, desperate, and heart wrenching all at the same time. He let go of my wrist and I climbed on him to position myself more properly. My hands were on either side of his head as I spread my legs apart and across his hips.

His palm immediately went to my crotch. "I told you to wear more dresses, " he rasped, breathless.

For once, I was remorseful. I broke away from his mouth to make the promise to him. "I'll be sure to do that throughout this week.

"And no panties either," he growled.

"Okay," I whispered.

With his eyes on me, he pulled at the button of my jeans and slipped his big, strong hand down into my panties and over my pussy. He palmed me hard.

A gasp of pleasure at the sweet pressure against my clit escaped my lips. My eyes shut as I savored the flick of his fingers on my slick folds.

Still holding onto me, he turned me around and put me on my back on the bed. He rose and began to unbutton his slacks.

My eyes widened in alarm. "Yuri, Yulia is just outside."

"We'll keep it down," he said.

Now, I panicked even more, because I had never been able to keep it down when we engaged in full sex.

He dug into his dark briefs and fetched his cock.

No matter how many times I saw it, it never failed to excite me. I gazed with unashamed lust at the beautiful shaft of his body but then shook my head to regain my senses. "I want to fuck you, Yuri more than you can imagine but we need to wait."

His hands were on my hips and pulling my jeans down.

"Yuri," I whispered desperately.

"No, I'm going to fuck you right here," he said. "I need to be inside of you right now.... I need to taste your sweet pussy, April." Pushing up my blouse he traced hard rapid kisses down my torso and then onto my sex.

The way he opened his mouth and covered my wet slick pussy made my back arch off the bed. I moaned feverishly as his tongue dug deep into my opening to lap up my juices, and his teeth nipped at my swollen, sensitive clit.

*"Yuri, please?"* I cried softly, but he refused to slow down.

His fingers joined the assault and I wanted to jump out of my skin. I kept a hand over my mouth, and the other on the duvet, tugging it violently to contain my sanity.

With rhythmic urgent thrusts, he finger-fucked me, his hand across my chest to pin me to the bed, while he ravished my pussy. I came with a maddened rush, my mouth opening in a cry. Thank God, his hand went over my mouth.

*Oh, my god. Oh, my fucking god.* My gaze hazed over as I was overcome by the waves upon waves of earth shattering ecstasy washing over me.

The captain's announcement came through the speakers as Yuri pounced on me. "Let's return back to earth with the plane," he said.

Somehow, I found the ability to laugh. I pulled him up to me to hide the tears that had pooled in my eyes and kissed him, my tongue dancing playfully with his as I savored the taste of my cum in his mouth. Soon he was poised at my entrance and I held my breath, my crazed pussy pulsing with emptiness and need, unable to wait for his possession.

He slammed into me, and all the nerves in my body tightened as he stretched and filled me the way no one else ever had. My walls milked his thick cock, greedily. He began to ram into me, his thrusts, hard and fast, and oh so sweet, I couldn't contain myself. *Yuri* I heard myself cry out. *"Ah, fuck , fuuuuc-"*

He crushed his lips to mine, and I realized how out of control I was.

"Keep your voice down," he said into my mouth.

The warning barely registered with me. I grabbed hold of his firm buttocks and rocked my hips against his, my legs encircling him so that I could take him as deep as possible. "Oh God," I cried hoarsely, as my body began to convulse.

*I missed you. I fucking missed you, Yuri Volkov.*

I came hard, as he pounded brutally on my clit to wrench every last bit of pleasure that he could get out of the delicious assault. My legs were flailing in all directions as I trembled, and when Yuri exploded in me, I nearly lost it. I took him, all of him and held on desperately to his neck. He kissed me burying his cries in me, and in that moment, I knew that there was no way the entire airplane wasn't aware of what was going on.

I couldn't have given less of a fuck, until I remembered Yulia. Even so, I couldn't let go of Yuri. I broke the kiss and buried my face in his neck, my brain as alive as the rest of my body.

He brushed my sweat plastered hair away from my forehead and gazed with amusement into my eyes.

I don't think that I'd ever seen him so light hearted. I was suddenly so shy, and tried to turn away but he wouldn't let me.

The captain's announcement came again and my eyes widened in realization.

"We've landed," he said with a laugh, as he slipped his cock out of me, slick with juices from us both.

# CHAPTER 39

## APRIL

Yulia was full of energy and bounce when we landed, while I on the other hand after being worn out by Yuri, was feeling lazy, almost in a dreamy state.

However, I didn't want to fall asleep. The light was fading as we arrived, but as we passed through the stone gates, I could already see that he'd really meant a chateau. *Whoa!* Made from yellow sandstone, it rose from the ground like something out of a fairytale.

The front doors were tall and imposing and more security men streamed out. We got out of the car and walked the steps to the entrance while Yuri and Alex went to talk to the men. As we stood at the front entrance waiting for them to join us, I looked around. For miles and miles around as far as the eye could see were vineyards and farmland. It was incredibly beautiful and serene. I could live here forever.

The foyer was at least thrice the size of the one in a London.

A stern-faced woman in a black dress came to meet us. She introduced herself as Lyudmila and asked if we wanted to explore the house first, or go straight to our bedrooms. I was too tired to explore so we climbed up a stone staircase and went to our rooms.

My bedroom gave off Louis the 15[th] vibes with huge tapestries, grand brocade curtains, and gilded furniture. A massive four-poster, canopied bed was perched on a wooden platform. I had never slept in one before and I gave a squeal of delight. I'd always dreamed of sleeping in one.

As soon as Lyudmila left, I looked at Yulia. "Shall we?"

She looked at me curiously.

Without saying a word, I ran to the bed, jumping on it then bounced up and down on the mattress.

With a big grin, she followed my example. We were really going for it when Yuri came in. Instantly, Yulia stopped.

"You want to go to your room now?" I asked her.

She nodded and walked away.

"Hey," I said almost shyly.

He moved closer and looked at me sitting cross-legged on the bed.

Suddenly I felt awkward. He'd just seen me behaving in a very childish way. "Um...how old is this place?" I asked as casually as I could.

"My grandfather bought it when my father was just a little boy and made renovations to the entire place. It dates back to the 16th century, I believe."

"Wow," I said my eyes studying the innate portraits on the

wall. "I know so little about the architecture of that century. There's so much to learn from here."

"Well, there's nothing at all to learn tonight. We need to take a shower."

I cocked my eyebrow as he moved closer. "We?"

"We," he repeated.

I couldn't stop the flush of pleasure that spread up my face. Playfully, I tried to roll off the bed so I would land on the other side, but he was too fast. He grabbed my leg and pulled me back to the edge. I burst into a laughter that was belly deep. He threw me over his shoulders and headed off into the bathroom. It was elegant, my eyes rounded at the stand-alone gold tub in the center of the room. Yup, no denying it, Russians sure liked their glitz.

He led me to the shower and began to tear at my clothes.

"Are we going to be just showering?" I asked cheekily.

"Of course not," he hissed, as he took my nipple in his mouth. "We have a week. The only time my cock is not going to be in your pussy is when you're asleep and even then there is the strong possibility I could try."

I couldn't stop my laughter. "I'm not going to be getting much sleep am I?"

"You can sleep when our week is over," he said as he brushed my hair gently out of my face. He was smiling, but his eyes looked desolate.

*Please don't look at me that way* I pleaded with him in my mind. Otherwise, this week would become the most tragic of my life. "I take it then that you won't be staying in your room much," I said as lightly as I could.

"This is *our* room," he said.

My eyes widened in shock. Before I could give any sort of protest, he slipped his tongue into my mouth, and I melted completely into his arms.

## CHAPTER 40

### APRIL

We made mad passionate love twice more during the night. I didn't want Yulia to find me in bed with her uncle, so I planned on waking up at nearly six in order to get into her bedroom by seven and explain to her.

I was afraid she might think it was a betrayal if I didn't explain the situation properly.

I opened my eyes and found his head was on my chest, cushioned against my breasts. He had his arm around my waist, almost locking me in place. I experienced a deep feeling of wonder fill my being, as I watched the gentle rise and fall of his chest. Asleep, he was glorious. Muscles rose and dipped down his back and at the base was the view of his round firm ass partially covered by the duvet tangled around his legs.

Time passed. I didn't want to break the connection. I stroked his hair, gently and kissed the top of his head as I sighed. I just didn't want to break the moment, until I remembered Yulia. I jumped then, and it startled him awake.

"I'm so sorry," I apologized, my heart fluttering madly as his blue eyes fixed on mine.

He stretched and my mouth hung open at the ripple of muscles. I began to pull myself away but he held me down.

Now, I was underneath his arms. "I need to go to Yulia. I don't want her to find out about us by seeing us in bed together."

"Don't worry your pretty little head. That's all be taken care of. Yulia has gone horseback riding with Alex. She left at six. You thought I'd let her interrupt me while I'm fucking you?"

"I should be so lucky." Vaguely irritated at the high-handed way he'd taken control, I began to push at him, but he wouldn't let me leave.

Instead, he poked his tongue into my navel and somehow it all became amusing. I collapsed into hysterical laughter. He joined me, his rich voice rolling across the room.

"Yuri," I murmured.

"Yes."

"I really just wanted to breathe, I'm not running away."

He leaned down to plant the softest of kisses on my forehead. Slowly, he traced kisses down my cheeks and to my jaw.

I was fast losing my train of thought, especially when I felt his cock harden against my thigh. "What are our plans for the day?"

"Very simple. I'm fucking you till ten. Then you have a two hours break. After which I want you to come to my study to be sucked off. You have another hour break then we have a picnic planned this afternoon in the vineyard."

"You have a vineyard?" I asked.

His mouth covered my nipple. "Mmm...80 hectares."

"Fuck," I said.

He came up chuckling. "Were you making a request, or expressing a comment about the size of my vineyard?"

"You're beautiful when you laugh," I whispered.

He laughed so hard that he got off me and collapsed on the bed beside me.

I took the chance and sat astride him, deliberately and slowly rubbing my pussy against his hard length. "What is so funny?" I asked.

"I've never been called beautiful."

"So what then are you called?"

His hands came up and curled around my hips. "The word I hear the most is bastard."

I stopped. "Is that literal?"

"It is not."

I carried on rubbing myself on him. "Then you must annoy people quite often."

"It's an occupational hazard," he dismissed, holding my gaze. "You're not going to answer my question?"

I gave him a profuse smile. "I meant the vineyard."

"Shame," he murmured, the smile slowly disappearing from his face. Holding me by the waist, he lifted me away from him.

I took his shaft in my hand and with my eyes on his, positioned it over my entrance.

Then he pushed me down onto the thick head of his cock, as his eyelids fluttered dreamily.

## CHAPTER 41

APRIL

An hour later and we were all seated on a large mat somewhere in the middle of the eighty hectares of vines. Yuri and I were beside each other while Yulia and Alex were opposite.

My idea of a picnic was cold chicken sandwiches, some cans of soda, and some cupcakes. What was on the mat was a lavish feast with platters of all kinds of meats, pasta, salad, pickled treats, bread, sweets, cakes, pastries, three bottles of rich red wine that the vineyard produced.

I gazed at Yuri as he opened a bottle of wine. This was the most relaxed I'd ever seen him in a pair of dark jeans and a loose white T-shirt. His hair was all over the place in light wind tousled waves, and his eyes were sparkling.

He poured a glass of Merlot for me and I lifted it to my lips. At the rich, mellow taste, I shut my eyes and nodded approvingly.

He laughed and quarter filled another glass with Petit Verdot. "This is a bit drier," he said.

Just before I took a sip, I glanced towards our audience.

Yulia looked like she was about to burst into tears while Alex just stared at Yuri with a disbelieving look in his eyes.

"Yulia are you okay?" I asked.

She dropped her gaze and picked disinterestedly at her food.

I turned to Yuri, and met him watching her too. With a touch to his arm, I silently urged him to speak to her.

"Yulia," he called.

She responded immediately by looking up at him, her face fearful.

I really couldn't understand why she was so afraid of him when he seemed not only to have such a deep love for her, but was also so protective of her.

Alex's phone began to ring then. He picked it up, his gaze on Yuri. He listened for a moment and then fired off some rapid Russian instructions before turning to Yuri then he said something to him, also in Russian.

Yuri frowned and nodded.

Both men rose to their feet. Yuri turned to Yulia and gave her a gentle smile. It changed his entire stern outlook.

Once, all I could see was a rude beast of man, now I saw through the cracks the bright light inside him.

"I'll be back soon," he said to me. "The afternoon was planned with a bicycle ride on the beach, but you can do that with Yulia."

I didn't want Yuri to leave. I could feel my heart sinking.

With a warm squeeze on my shoulder, he strolled away with Alex and I hoped whatever it was he was going to he wouldn't return in a bad mood.

I turned to Yulia and decided to speak frankly with her since we were alone. I had only a few more days left and I needed to get to the root of this intense fear she had of her uncle. "Honey," I called and she raised her head to me. "Are you all right?"

She nodded.

"Will you tell me if something was wrong?"

She thought about it then nodded slowly.

"Are you afraid of your uncle?"

She swallowed hard and swung her head to look at the departing men.

"Are you?" I prompted.

She bit her lip.

"You can tell me. I promise I won't tell anyone."

Slowly, she nodded her head.

"Can you tell me why?"

Suddenly, her eyes filled with tears.

It broke my heart to see how hurt she was. I reached over and pulled her into my arms. "It's okay. Don't cry. Whatever it is we'll work it out together, okay?"

She didn't say a word after that, so slightly frustrated, I let it go.

Finally, after a while we were done eating.

One of the workers, named Anton came and smiled at us. He had leathery face and he wore a cap. "Do you both want to pick some grapes?"

I looked at Yulia and my heart warmed when her excitement seemed to be returning.

Half an hour later, we were below vines of grapes and eating more than we were harvesting. I took a little water bottle with me so whenever Yulia wanted to slip one in her mouth she brought it over and I washed it for her. They were fat, richly colored and extremely sweet.

I didn't want them to upset Yulia's stomach, so we handed over our fruits to Anton. After that, we went with Brain and two other security staff to the beach.

"The chateau is close to the Omaha beach," Anton said.

I was already exhausted but I could see that Yulia's whole face had lit up. Two bicycles were brought to us, a tiny pink one for her. We cycled along the beach, then we stopped at a cove and swam and played in the sand. It was wonderful spending time with Yulia, but all the time my thoughts kept drifting back to Yuri.

The sun was hot and both of us were near falling asleep. By the time we returned to the chateau, my body was hurting a little bit more than usual and I fell on my bed and fell almost immediately asleep.

# CHAPTER 42

## YURI

It was almost midnight when I returned. I'd wanted to spend as much of the day with April and Yulia, but unscheduled urgent meetings had kept Alex and I occupied for most of the day.

I didn't want to turn on the light, so I took a quick shower and turned in. I laid down beside her, my heart beating just a little bit too fast. Spending last night with April had been the best sleep I'd had in as long as I could remember. The windows were open, so the cool summer breeze could come in, but when I pulled her into my arms, I found her body was burning up and she was covered in sweat.

"April," I called.

She came awake and smiled, a sweet, innocent smile.

It went straight to my heart.

"Yuri?" she whispered.

"You're burning up'"

She lay her head on my chest. "It's nothing. I always get fevers for no reason. I'll sleep it off," she said, drowsily. "I'll be fine tomorrow."

The next morning came and a doctor had to be called. Her fever didn't go down during the night despite the cold cloth I continuously ran all over her body.

"I'm fine," she said to me with a flushed face and a weakened tone. "This is nothing. I've ridden out worse fevers than this. It's probably just too much sun. I usually get better after taking a couple of painkillers."

I sighed. The casual way she was dismissing her illness made me think of her foster upbringing. "How hard was growing up for you?"

She shrugged. "Hard is not the word I would use. I moved around a lot. And I was angry a lot. That's what I remember most. Oh, and I also felt abandoned a lot, but you know... I didn't take it personally, at least I tried not to." She shrugged again. "I told you before that my mom gave me up when I was Yulia's age, right?" She looked directly at me.

I nodded. This wasn't the time to tell her that I'd done some research and found her mother and she was the mother of the woman who tried to sit next to me at Grosvenor House Hotel.

"Basically," she continued, "I was ruining her life. Her parents had kicked her out for having me so early, so she was really struggling. I didn't really hold it against her, but when I found out that things got better for her, a lot better, and yet she never bothered to check up on me, or even look for me, that really hurt." She swallowed hard as she paused.

In this moment, I wanted to kill that shallow creature who had abandoned her.

"I was about thirteen and I'd just been moved away again out of a foster home for no reason. That was when I decided I wasn't going to move again, or depend on anyone else. It was easy to not be adopted when you were a raging bitch to everyone. So I played the part of hateful little bitch until the day I met Charlotte. Remember her? She was the one who opened the door when you came to our apartment."

I nodded. Sure, I remembered the blonde.

"I don't know what the hell she saw in me but from the first day we met, she decided I was going to be her very best friend. I don't think I even had a choice. In time, she became the sister I never had."

I could hear a slight break in her voice, so I rubbed gently down her back.

She turned to search for my eyes. "That was a long answer to a short question, wasn't it? I'm sorry."

I ran my fingers through her hair. "I don't mind. Alex is that way to me. I lost my mother when I was a kid too." I hesitated. I wondered whether to just gloss over it all, but then I decided to just say it as it was. I'd never spoken to anyone about it, but even if it all ended in a week with April, I wanted her to know my biggest secret. "My dad killed her."

April went completely still.

"She was cheating on him so he just strangled her to death right in front of me. I hated him for it until the day he died. He disposed of the body and pretended to everyone that she had run back to Russia. He got away with her murder. For years, I wondered if Karma would get him. It took its own sweet time, but it did. He suffered for nearly two years with cancer. By the time he died, the disease had worn him down to a skeleton. There was so little flesh on his face left, even his corpse bore the expression of a terrible grimace. On his deathbed, he cried. Fucking bastard wanted to carry on living even with all that pain. I gave him a lavish funeral, but I didn't shed a fucking tear."

She snuggled even further into me trying to provide as much comfort as she could and it made breathing a little easier. "You and Alex are really close too?"

"Having Alex by my side when I was growing up made it all easier, so I more than understand your connection to Charlotte."

"You know there's a saying that goes around in your household, that he is the only one you listen to," she said.

I smiled. "Really?"

"Yeah, and I understand why that would be the case, but when I mentioned it to him, he confused me even further."

"Why, what did he say?"

"He said, Yuri listens to everyone. I'm still not exactly sure what he meant by that."

"Me neither," I said. "One would hope that with how little he speaks he would at least make himself clear, but he's law unto himself. For the most part, he can't be bothered what people think of him."

"What about his family?" she asked.

I scowled.

April immediately rushed to apologize. "I'm sorry if that's too personal."

"No, it's not that. I'm just wondering how much to say. In my world, less is always more. His mother moved with him from Canada to London when he was about ten. All I can say is that he has no need to be by my side. His family is fabulously wealthy, but the fact that he chose to... It maybe a little farfetched for you all to say that I only listen to him, but there is some truth in there. I do listen to him. I'm hot tempered and rash and he keeps me on the straight and narrow. "

She sighed. "I wish Charlotte was that sane. If I listened to all she said, I'd probably be in jail by now, or something. She's insane, most of the time."

I laughed and tightened my arms around her. My phone began to ring and I picked it up to see that it was Alex. "Great. Your doctor's here," I informed her.

She groaned aloud. "I don't need a doctor."

"Don't be a baby." I threw the covers away from her and found her a pair of shorts from one of the drawers she had unpacked her luggage into. I tugged her by the legs to the edge of the bed and started to pull the shorts up her legs, but I just couldn't resist the lure of her blue panties. Stopping at her knees, I pushed my head forward and covered her sweet pussy with my mouth.

"This is not how you treat someone who's ill," she whimpered.

"It's just an incentive for you to get better quickly," I said before taking a nip of her clit through the lacy material. I had intended to stop, but I soon got carried away when her hips started squirming in response to my mouth.

Her breathing was hard and heavy, but just as I began to roll the panties off her hips there was a knock to the door.

I stilled then, but she wrapped her legs around me, holding me in place. "No," she said, "I'm fine. I don't need a doctor. Send him away and carry on with what you're doing."

I wrestled her legs away from me and slipped the shorts on her. "Come in," I called. Just as I threw the covers over her, the doctor came in, along with the housekeeper.

I sat by the bedside as he examined her.

When he was done checking her over, his diagnosis was simple. “She's showing symptoms of heat stroke. But with a few days of rest indoors, she should be better with time." He prescribed some drugs for her and went on his way.

“Onion soup and French bread is on its way to you,” I said.

She reached up to kiss me. "I can't stay in bed for too long, so please don't force me to. I’ve never been to France before and apart from this opportunity, I don't know when next I'll get the chance. I want to explore the city with Yulia and you."

"Well, get better quickly then, and you will get to."

# CHAPTER 43

## APRIL

I did get better and we did have a great time exploring the caves around the beach and going into the little town having French food in bistros, but then Yuri had to leave two days earlier for an urgent appointment in Venice, and I was left with Yulia. If I was going to leave, it had to be the next day. Otherwise, I would never have the guts to make that painful decision. I packed my bags during the night, but I couldn't sleep so I called Charlotte.

"Have you told Yulia?" she asked.

I shook my head trying to hold back the grief that wanted to overwhelm me.

"You're shaking your head, are you? I can't see you, you dummy you," she stated.

The insult somehow brought a smile out of me. "No, I haven't," I answered with a sigh. "I'll do that tomorrow morning."

"What about *him?*"

"He left ahead of us. All he said was that he would see us back in London."

"How was your week with him?"

I told the truth, and this time I couldn't hold back the tears. "I'm think I'm love with him."

"So why are you leaving?"

"I can't see clearly with Yuri. For starters, his world is not one I could ever be fully a part of. And I know he cares about me, but how far is he willing to go?"

"Have you asked him about any of this?"

"So that I can shatter my heart more than it already is?"

She didn't say a word.

"I shouldn't have agreed to this one week. It was a fucking mistake."

"Did you enjoy your time with him?"

"I never wanted it to end."

"But now reality is calling. If I were you, I would stay and damn the consequences to hell, but that's where we're different. You didn't grow up using your heart because you didn't have the luxury. It had to be ignored so that you could see through the hurt. I understand that, but even so, don't you think a broken heart is worth risking for this beautiful thing you have."

"Oh God, what do I do Charlotte?"

"I can't tell you what to do, babe. You know what I would do. I would only leave when leaving is no longer a choice."

"What do you mean?"

"I mean I'd go when leaving is the only option on the table. Then no matter what happens, I'd never regret my choice."

I fell asleep with Charlotte's words echoing in my ears, but I realized I wasn't Charlotte. I couldn't play around with my heart. Wait until there was no option but to leave? The next morning, I went in Yulia's room, sat her down on her bed while I sat on the floor in front of her so I could look into her eyes.

Her smile was so sweet and so unsuspecting that I almost didn't continue with my announcement. For a while, I was unable to speak. Then I took a deep breath. Yulia had Yuri to take care of her, I had only me to take care of me. "Listen honey, I've loved being your nanny so much. You don't know how much. You are such a beautiful, amazing girl, but I need to leave."

Her smile died. She looked desperately around for her pad and pen.

The moment I saw tears fall from her eyes, I turned my face away to hide mine. I quickly dried my eyes and turned back to see what she scribbled almost illegibly on the pad.

Why?

How was I to explain my heart to this little girl?

Is it Uncle Yuri?

My heart hammered in my chest. I shook my head. "No, no, of course not. Your uncle has been very kind to me." I sighed.

There was no way she could understand that I couldn't go against the one person I had vowed to protect at all costs —*myself*. It would sound exactly the way it was, selfish and without much concern for her wellbeing.

"I'll get you another nanny," I promised desperately. "Someone much better than myself. You'll love her I promise—"

She gave a shriek of fury and pain then. When I tried to pull her into my arms, she wouldn't let me touch her, so I sat there without a clue on what to do. I was terrified beyond words that I was harming her permanently. I wished I hadn't told her now. I should have waited until we got back to London.

She wouldn't stop crying, so eventually I rose to my feet. Perhaps my absence would calm her down just a little. It broke my heart to leave her, but I didn't know what else to do. Just as I made it to the door, for the very first time since I had stepped foot in their home, I heard her voice.

"April," she cried out.

I *froze*. At first, I was sure my ears were playing tricks with me, so I spun around to meet her gaze.

Her face was soaked with tears. "Don't go, please? I'm scared."

My knees nearly buckled. Somehow, I made my way over to her. I sat on the bed and pulled her to me. "Yulia, you can speak," was all that I could say.

"I could always speak," she said.

I wiped the tears from her face. "What's going on?"

"He killed my parents," she said, barely able to catch her breath as the tears came pouring down her face.

"What do you mean?"

"Uncle killed them," she cried.

I held my breath, almost too afraid to ask. "Which Uncle?"

"Uncle Yuri," she replied.

I gasped as my heart fell into my stomach.

## CHAPTER 44

### APRIL

Naturally, I didn't leave the child in France.

I came back with her to London. I was in a state of devastated shock. I didn't want to believe it. I couldn't believe it. I had bared my heart to him. I trusted him. He told me about his mother. It couldn't be.

A thousand thoughts and possibilities swirled through my head, but they all hinged on the only truth I would accept. That Yulia was mistaken. Yuri was dangerous, in more ways than I wanted to fathom, but there was no way I was going to accept that the man I had fallen for was heartless enough to murder his own brother and sister-in-law in cold blood.

Even so, I couldn't deny that whatever Yulia knew, had been severe and devastating enough that she'd become speechless through sheer terror and will for almost half a year.

I asked her if she could be mistaken, but she told me she could prove it, if I just called her Grand uncle Ivan. For the sake of Yulia, we found his number and called him to come to the house. I sat on the floor in a corner of the room and watched as he came into the room.

Immediately, Yulia ran into his arms.

My eyes followed Ivan as he sat on the edge of the couch. "Is it true?" I asked him.

Gravely, he nodded in response and my head lowered to the floor. My brain refused to give my heart a pass.

"It happened in Yulia's parents' home in Surrey. Yulia's father and Yuri got in an atrocious fight in his study. It was so severe that her mother came in with a gun, and forced Yuri out of the room. The surveillance video showed that Yuri came back and shot the both of them dead."

My head was close to exploding but I forced myself to keep calm. "A video?"

"That was how Yulia found out. One of my men is in Yuri's camp, so when he saw the video he recorded it with his phone, and sent it to me through the sleeve of one of Yulia's stuffed animals. We couldn't retrieve it in time before Yulia fiddled with the phone and saw it. When I came by to meet Yuri, I got her alone and found out what had happened."

I looked at Yulia. "She's just a child. How was she able to hold on this long without saying a word?"

"That's what amazed me too. It must have scarred her so terribly. I've been working to gather enough evidence to take Yuri down, so she agreed to hold on. She stopped speaking because she didn't want to accidentally let the cat out of the bag. I'm so surprised she spoke up now. It seems that she trusts you a whole lot."

I felt so cold, that I wrapped my arms around myself. "Why do you need to gather more evidence? Isn't the video already more than enough?"

"You do not know Yuri, do you?" he asked.

I looked up to meet the unbridled fear in his eyes.

"At the mere word of a video he will find a way to instantly get rid of it, and even if it somehow, makes its way to the authorities, his entire empire is in cohorts with the highest people in power. You should have realized by now that he is no ordinary man."

I returned my eyes to the floor. "He is no ordinary man but neither is he this inhumanely cruel."

"April, things happen that none of us ever intend, and moreover for the right price, anyone can turn inhumanely cruel."

I thought back to what Yuri had said to me about his mother's death. He hadn't delved into detail but I knew that it was not a path that he would willing have gone down also.

"But he loves Yulia," I defended. "So very much. Why would he do that if he knew—"

"Guilt," Ivan interrupted. "He is brutal. You are right in that he is not heartless, but what was at stake is his brother's empire which is almost as vast as his own. A little guilt doesn't seem much of a price to pay."

He had all the answers, but none of it was what I wanted to hear so I sunk into my own thoughts, my body beginning to tremble.

But he wasn't finished. "Right now, the only way he can get access to his brother's vast fortune is through Yulia, so of course he has to care and keep her safe. If anything at all happened to her, the entire estate becomes a charitable trust."

I thought back to how Yuri had over-reacted just because I had taken Yulia out of the house with me. Had that been not just out of care for her safety then? I shut my eyes. "So what do we do now?" I asked.

His answer came, "Just go on as though nothing happened. If Yuri even gets a whiff of our knowledge of any of this, then we will all be in trouble. If it's too much for you to handle then just quit the job and walk away."

Jesus, pretend as if nothing has happened? No wonder, little Yulia took the path of refusing to speak.

There was a noise of a vehicle arriving outside and three of us turned towards the window.

Ivan hurried over to the window and when he turned back, his eyes were filled with panic. "Yuri's here."

"He's not supposed to be back until tomorrow," I whispered.

Yulia instantly shot up to her feet. I watched her and now it all made sense. Her fear and instant change of mood every time Yuri walked into the room.

"Yulia return to your bedroom," he said and but she didn't move. He came to me, crouched down and pulled out a gun from behind him. "Hold onto this," he said. "I'll be right back."

I gazed at the dark cold metal in alarm, but just before I could ask what the hell I was supposed to do with it, he was out of the door. A few moments later, he hurried back in, tucking in I was certain another pistol behind him. "Yuri is on his way here," he said to me.

"Why the hell do I need this?" I asked in a shaky voice.

"Most of the rooms in this house are monitored. He might have already caught on to what is going on."

"That doesn't answer my questio—"

The door was pushed open and Yuri stood there. He looked around the room at the three of us and said four simple words. "Yulia and April, *leave*."

She instantly broke into tears and ran to me, wrapping her arms around my neck, refusing to let go. I rose to my feet then. Things happened really quickly after that.

Ivan suddenly drew out the weapon from behind him and pointed it directly at Yuri.

"No!" I screamed before I could hold myself back.

Yuri's eyes were glued on Ivan. "What the fuck are you doing in my house?"

Ivan turned towards us. "April take Yulia out of the room." His voice was cold steel. When I hesitated, he roared with a bone chilling urgency, "Right now! Use the gun I gave you, don't let anyone stop either of you. There'll be a car waiting downstairs."

Yuri turned to me then at the mention of a gun. "April, I haven't given my security any instructions," he said. "The moment they catch sight of a gun you are finished. Don't you dare leave this room."

"April get out of here, right now!" Ivan yelled.

I had never been so torn, as I looked between him and Yuri.

Ivan went on, "Do you want to ruin Yulia's life? This fucking bastard killed her parents."

Yuri turned to me then. "Is that what this scum told you? And you believed him?"

"There's a video," I said.

"Did you see the video?" he asked.

"Yulia saw it, that's why she hasn't spoken for the past six months."

Yuri looked devastated his gaze centered on me.

I couldn't stand it. I was weakening, so I pulled out the gun and pointed it at him.

"It's very easy to deceive a child with a video, April. Children don't know what can be done with photoshop," he said to me.

Now things clicked into place.

I took my first real breath in God knew how long as I finally received the only answer I was searching for. My hands were shaking when I whirled around unsteadily and pointed the gun at Ivan.

His eyes shot open in shock. "What the fuck are you doing?"

"I believe Yuri," I said.

Yulia began to pull at my legs. "April no!" she wailed.

I turned a stern gaze to her. "Do you trust me?"

She nodded.

"Good. Go to your bed right now and pull the covers over your head."

She stared at me silently.

"Go!" I screamed at her.

Wailing, she refused to move.

I supported the gun with both hands, wishing in that moment more than anything in the world, that I had listened to Yuri when he'd told me to at least learn how to use the gun. Hopefully, I would somehow be able to escape here today without killing myself.

"April put the gun down and take Yulia to her room," Yuri said.

I turned a helpless gaze to him. "What about you?"

"I'll handle myself. This fucking coward will not dare shoot me."

I shook my head. I felt almost giddy with fear and shock. "You take Yulia out of here."

Yuri took a step forward and Ivan fired a shot that somehow missed Yuri. I screamed, and so did Yulia."

"You think I'm fucking joking, don't you?" Ivan bellowed. "Take another step and the bullet will go straight through your head, or maybe..." He turned the pistol towards me.

My palms were sweating, hands trembling, and my eyes were too afraid even to blink. I thought my legs would give out on me

"She's the one you really want to protect, isn't she?" His gaze on me was angry. "You fucked him didn't you?" Ivan spat.

"Stupid bitch. I should have known. I hope your betrayal haunts you. You're destroying Yulia's life."

"You're the one who wants to destroy her life right now," I yelled. "Put your fucking gun down!" I was angry, at the terror he was subjecting Yulia to, however it manifested as streams of hot tears that ran down my face and almost kept Ivan out of focus. I was now resigned to the worst, and no matter what happened, I knew that I wouldn't regret the decisions I made in this room because they came out of the purity of my heart.

The door behind me flung open with a bang, and my heart nearly left my chest. At the deafening fire of a gun, I screamed and turned to see that Yuri had been hit, and then I don't know how I did it, but I managed to fire my own gun. I shut my eyes and collapsed to the floor, shaking and wailing, unsure of what had just happened.

I would never know how many minutes went by, but it felt as though the world had collapsed at my feet. A hand eventually touched my shoulder and I opened my eyes to see Alex.

I looked up in shock at him and then turned to see two bodies on the ground. Ivan had been shot straight through the heart, and was unmoving. Jesus, I was a good shot.

Yuri was leaning against the wall his hand on his shoulder. Underneath a wound was rapidly spreading crimson blood all over his white shirt.

"Yuri!" I screamed and ran to him.

He bared his teeth in a ferocious smile. "You did good."

Just hearing his voice almost made me pass out with relief. "Are you all right?"

He shook his head. “No, but I will be.”

A team of his guards came in then with a gurney, and he was laid onto it.

The pain on his face was too excruciating for me to bear. I turned my face away and suddenly remembered Yulia. I glanced around the room. She was nowhere to be seen. “Where’s Yulia?” I asked urgently.

Alex responded, his eyes still on Yuri, “I took her out. She’s fine.”

I went with Yuri and got into his waiting SUV, and we were sped to the hospital. I didn’t know how I was still functioning, but he held unto my hands as they sped along and I buried my face in his neck.

“I’ll be fine,” he said to me. “I promise you.”

I managed to get out some words, “You better be, or I’ll kill you otherwise, I swear to God. Please.”

He was taken in immediately for an operation, then I collapsed, spent and haunted by the ordeal of a lifetime, in the corridor of the hospital. Not until he was somewhat stabilized did I eventually come to my senses.

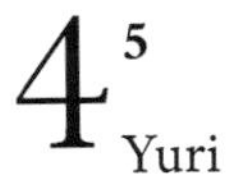

## 5

### Yuri

https://www.youtube.com/watch?v=ZMuMmQtGvOQ

I Ran Out Of That Grave

I was awake a few hours after my operation.

I opened my eyes to see the face of an angel. My angel, seated beside me, her head lying on the bed, and one hand holding mine. She seemed to be asleep, and I didn't want to wake her, but the moment I tried to move my hand even just a little, she came awake.

At first, she seemed disoriented, but then she registered that I was conscious, and her eyes nearly popped out of their sockets. "Yuri," she gasped and came closer to me, her hands touching my face gently to feel for my temperature. "Are you okay? How do you feel?"

"I'm fine. It's not the first time I've been shot.

I could see that those words brought absolutely no comfort whatsoever to her, so I quickly apologized. "I'm sorry," I said and brushed her hair away from her face.

April lowered her head to my chest and tried to hold back her tears.

"Thank you for believing me," I said quietly to her. "I've been aware of Ivan's hand in the murder of Yulia's parents for quite a while. I had left the room after the argument, and returned at the sound of shots to see both of them lying on the floor, dead. The video was most probably edited for Yulia to make it seem like I was the one who returned and killed the both of them. And the corpse you saw at the construction yard was the one who drove the killers away that night."

She remained silent as she watched me, still so visibly shaken. "Why would he do such a horrible thing?" she croaked out.

"Yulia is the sole benefactor of her father's estate, and it is worth almost three billion pounds. The only way to get access to any of that is through Yulia. My uncle knew that I would never, under any circumstances let that happen, but if Yulia thought that I was the one who killed her parents, then perhaps she would lean against him instead and once he got rid of me, she would be happy to give him full control. The cops have been investigating this for a while with me now. I had nothing to fear. My businesses are all legit or watertight protected. So I agreed to help them. They knew Ivan was involved in some way, they will be glad to see the video of what happened at home with Ivan…Now kiss me." I needed to know that we were okay, and that she wasn't going to leave.

She gazed at me for a little while, and then she came for me, her lips crushing mine in an almost desperate, teary-eyed kiss.

"I've got one more confession."

She drew back slightly. "What is it?"

"That night I took you to Grosvenor House Hotel, I knew your mother would be there and I was hoping you would be able to patch it."

Her eyes widened. "You knew who my mother was?"

"Yeah." I grimaced. "I had someone do some digging. I was trying to help. I thought it would be a great reunion. I guess, I didn't expect it to become the fiasco it did."

She shrugged. "I'm glad it happened that way. All my life I was chasing a dream, finally, I saw it for what it was. After that night I stopped chasing that empty promise and now I'm just grateful for all the wonderful things that I actually have around me. Charlotte, Yulia...you..."

"I'm still sorry you had to go through that public humiliation though," I apologized. "I swear I will *never* allow anything like that to happen to you again." With my good arm, I held her to me, refusing to let go. I took a deep breath. "And now for the big declaration. April Winters, please don't leave me," I rasped out. "I want you in my life. I love you. I think I've loved you for a long time, but I didn't want to accept it."

Her eyes grew round with wonder. "You love me?"

"Yes, I fucking love you and anyway, what would I do without my little wild cat?"

She stilled against my chest.

I held my breath as she pulled away from me.

She looked into my eyes. "I'm not going anywhere, my love. It would be too hard to leave a man you are so crazy in love with that you'd kill another human being for and die for if necessary."

My eyes filled with tears. "God, how I love you, April."

# EPILOGUE

## APRIL

***16 months later***

https://www.youtube.com/watch?v=PQBW6G0hSrs
(Speak Softly Love)

"I hate you."

I smiled at the statement as Charlotte adjusted the bejeweled tiara on my head.

"I'll never forgive you for this. You have access to billions and this is the wedding you chose? A quiet remote Scottish castle and a chapel? Aren't Russians supposed to be big spenders who love to show off?"

"You know me, Charlotte. I like things simple," I murmured, more amused than offended. "This is what we both want."

"Whatever," she concluded. When she was done, she turned me around so I could see myself in the long mirror.

"I'm getting married, Charlotte," I whispered, looking at myself in awe.

"If you aren't, then you're sure going to look silly in that get-up in the church," she quipped.

I smiled. "You're crazy."

"Tell me something I don't know. Come on Cinderella, time to meet the Prince."

We walked together until we got to the entrance of the beautiful chapel in Dornoch, and joined my handful of bridesmaids and flower girls. Charlotte turned to me. "Go get him, tiger."

And for a moment, I felt a pang of sadness for Charlotte. I was leaving her. She was the most beautiful person I knew. She'd seen me through ups and downs and she had no one. "Your turn will come soon," I said softly.

Yulia ran up to me then, looking angelic in her flowing white dress and flower crown.

I lowered myself down to her height.

"You look beautiful April," she said.

I placed a kiss on her cheeks, tears slowly gathering in my eyes.

When I rose, I was immediately rebuked. "Not today," Charlotte scolded. "We did that last night and this morning. No more tears, you're marrying the man of your dreams."

"I know," I said, unable to contain my joy. "I'm so happy, and terrified. What will the future hold?"

"Billions...er...I mean joy," she said with a laugh as she gently patted the corners of my eyes dry. "Unending joy and happiness. Yuri will make sure of that."

This answer chased all my fears away. "He will." I smiled and turned.

Charlotte's uncle came in then and offered me his arm.

With gratitude, I slipped my arm through and Charlotte fell in behind.

The music began and I was ushered ever so gracefully into the small private chapel. It wasn't full, but beyond beautiful. Yuri and I had taken care to only invite the people that really meant something in our lives. Those who had touched and cared for us in one way or the other, along our journey to eventually finding each other.

So although the castle was packed with the press waiting to record the wedding of one of the most desired bachelors in the world, inside were only our closest friends and guardians.

I lifted my gaze to meet Yuri's at the end of the aisle, and my heart swelled with so much love and pride it felt as if it would burst. He was breathtaking, and I almost couldn't walk fast enough. Dressed in an impeccable dark suit and vest, with his hair brushed away from his face, I felt the tears rush back to my eyes.

My man. He was beautiful, in every way possible.

Charlotte's uncle handed me over to him, and I placed my

hand in his. We said our vows. I never once looked away from the magic of his eyes. Then Yuri drew me in for a long, deep kiss. The church faded, the world dropped away. There was no one else, but us. Just us. Our mouths, our bodies, and our hearts beating together.

When he eventually pulled away, I was breathless. The church came back into my consciousness. I heard the applause of the entire chapel.

"I love you, Mrs. Volkov," he whispered to me. "With all of my heart. Thank you for choosing me."

I pulled him into my arms, and spoke the words I knew deep down in my soul, "I love you more, Mr. Volkov. Thank *you* for choosing me."

**THE END**

Yes, Charlotte gets her HEA too. :)
Set in a castle in Wales, hers is the next story.
Look out for:
**The Man In The Mirror**

In the meantime, if you're into gorgeous billionaire Russian Mafia bosses, here are some sample chapters from:
You Don't Own Me

## CHAPTER 1 (SAMPLE)

## DAHLIA FURY

'Oh, my God, Dahlia, you have to help me,' Stella, my best friend and roomie cries. She has burst open my bedroom door and is standing at the threshold theatrically wringing her hands.

Stella is a well-known drama queen so I don't panic. I mute my video and turn towards her. 'Calm down and tell me what's wrong.'

'I have a massage client in less than an hour and I've just realized that I've also got another client coming here.'

See what I mean about drama. 'Just cancel one of them,' I suggest reasonably.

'I can't do that. The one who is coming here is that crazy rich bitch from Richmond who told me she is going to recommend me to all her crazy assed rich friends in Richmond. She's probably already on the train. And the other is a Russian Mafia boss.'

I frown. First of all, I didn't know she had a Russian mafia boss as one of her clients. Must address that one later, but not yet. 'So what do you want me to do?'

'Can you stand in for me?'

I shake my head resolutely. 'Nope. Absolutely not. You'll just have to tell the Mafia boss that you can't make it.'

'I can't do that,' she wails. 'One of the clauses in the confidentiality agreement I signed was that I would never miss any of my appointments once I agreed it unless it was a life or death situation.'

'Huh?' I cock an eyebrow. 'He made you sign a confidentiality agreement?'

She makes an exasperated sound. 'Yes.'

'What kind of person puts an unreasonable clause like that into an agreement with their *masseuse*?' I ask, genuinely surprised.

'Dahlia,' she screams in frustration. 'Can you focus, please. I'm running out of time here.'

'It's simple. Go on to the Mafia boss, and I'll tell your other client when she arrives that she can have a free massage next week.'

'No, she can't come next week. She is away, and anyway, she's in pain and really needs me.'

'So tell the Mafia boss that you can't make it because you have a life and death scenario.'

'You want me to lie to Zane?' she asks incredulously.

'If that's what his name is,' I reply coolly.

She comes into the room and starts pacing the small space like a caged animal. 'I'm not going to lie to him. He'll know.' She stops and stares at me. 'He's got like the coldest most piercing eyes you ever saw. It's like they can see right through you.'

I laugh. 'I can't believe you said that.'

'I'm serious, Dahlia. Lying to him is out of the question.'

'Well, then you'll have to let the rich bitch down.'

'Did you not hear me? She's in pain. Oh, please, please, can you help me this time. You can have my fee and I'll owe you big time.'

'No,' I say clearly. The solution to her problem seems obvious to me —she should cancel the Russian guy.

'I'll do the dishes for a whole month,' she declares suddenly.

I pause. Hmmm. Then I shake my head.

'I'll do the dishes and clean the apartment for a whole month.'

I hesitate. 'Even the bathroom?'

'Yes, even the bathroom,' she confirms immediately.

'I'd love to help but—'

'Two months,' she says with a determined glint in her eyes.

My eyebrows fly upwards. I open my mouth and she shouts out, 'Three fucking months.'

To say that I am not tempted would be a lie. I HATE cleaning the bathroom. I am very tempted, but I can't actually take her up on her offer even if she offered me a year's worth of bathroom cleaning.

'Jesus, Stella. Just stop. You know I'd love to take you up on your offer, but I simply can't massage like you. I just about know the basics and rich bitch's problem sounds complicated. For all I know, I'll just end up making her back worse and instead of giving you a glowing recommendation to all her rich friends she will do the opposite.'

Stella fixes her hazel eyes on me. 'I wasn't thinking of her.'

I look at her, astonished 'What?'

'He just needs a simple basic Swedish. Just exactly what I've already taught you. You just need to put a bit more effort into it. He likes it really hard.'

'Like hell, I'm massaging your Mafia boss.'

She falls to her knees. 'Oh please, please, please.'

'If you're trying to make me feel guilty, it's not working,' I say.

She looks at me pleadingly. 'Pleeeeeeease. I promise you he's really easy to do.'

'Oh yeah. Is that why you're so terrified of him?'

She turns her mouth downwards. 'I'm not terrified of him.'

'Could have fooled me.'

She sighs. 'Actually, I'm a bit ... in lust with him,' she confesses with a wry smile.

'A bit? You?' I explode in disbelief. This is Stella, the woman who turns a spider sighting in her bedroom into a shrieking Victorian melodrama.

'Yeah,' she says softly.

'In lust?'

'Yeah.'

I shake my head in wonder. 'Since when?'

'Since,' she shrugs, 'forever. I've always had a thing for him, but of course, he's way out of my league. The women he dates are all at least ten feet tall and totally perfect. I only register on his radar as a pair of strong hands.'

I stare at her suspiciously. 'Are you just making all this up so I'll go and massage him?'

She shakes her head. 'No.'

'Why haven't you told me about this man crush before?'

She looks down at her right shoe. 'There seemed to be no point. I've come to terms with it. The truth is it is way stronger than a crush, and it could even be love, but there's nothing I can do about it.'

Suddenly I realize why every time we go out she freezes out every man, even the ones that look like serious contenders, who come up to her. 'Oh, Stella!' I breathe. I had no idea she was suffering in silence.

She looks at me sadly. 'It doesn't matter. It'll pass, but right now I just need your help. I don't want to let him down or give him cause to fire me. Until I'm ready to let go of him I want to keep this job going.'

'But—'

She holds up her hand. 'Don't say it. I know. It's stupid and it's crazy, and I don't know where I'm going with this, but I can't let go. Not yet. One day I'll eventually leave, I know that, but just not quite yet, OK?'

'OK.'

One corner of her mouth lifts. 'So you'll do it?'

Now I am torn between feeling horribly sorry for her and not wanting to be manipulated into massaging her Russian. 'I do want to help, Stella, but I can't. I'm not qualified. I wouldn't know what to do or say to someone like that.'

'You don't even have to talk to him. He never says a word. Just comes in and lies there, and after I've finished, I turn down the lights and leave. He doesn't even lift up his head to say goodbye.'

Ugh, sounds like a horrible man. I have a sinking feeling in my stomach. 'I think this is a really bad idea,' I say, but my voice is weak. Both of us know that she has won.

'Yes, you can. It's a plain massage. Nothing fancy. Just basic moves. You could do it with your eyes closed. All you have to remember is that he likes it hard.'

I stare at her indecisively.

'Remember three months of no cleaning.'

'Stella,' I groan.

'Oh, thank you. Thank you. I promise you'll never regret it. I owe you one.'

I sigh. 'I'm already regretting it.'

'Come on. Let's get you into one of my uniforms.'

We go into her room and I take my T-shirt off and slip into her white uniform. It has a black collar and black buttons all the way down, but because my boobs are so much bigger than hers I cannot button all the way.

'Now what?' I ask.

Her head disappears into her closet. She comes out with a scarf, hooks it around the back of my neck and tucks it into the front of her uniform.

I look at myself in the mirror.

'I really don't know about this, Stella,' I say doubtfully.

'Are you kidding? You absolutely look the part.'

'Are you mad? This uniform is too tight.'

'No, no, you look great,' she says quickly and bundles me out of her room. 'Look, you best get going or you'll be late. The car will be here anytime now.' She grabs my handbag from the dining table, presses it into my hands and practically pushes me out of the front door. Holding on to my elbow she rushes me down the corridor.

'Does he even know that I'm going in your place?'

'Not yet. Noah's phone was engaged, but I'll call again in a bit.'

We go into the lift together and as she said, there is a black Mercedes with tinted windows waiting outside. She opens the back door and manhandles me into it.

'See you later,' she calls cheerily as she closes the door with a thick click.

The driver glances at me in the mirror.

'You all right, Miss?'

'Yeah, I'm all right,' I say with a sigh. Looks like I'm massaging the man Stella is in love with.'

## CHAPTER 2 (SAMPLE)

### DAHLIA FURY

The Mafia boss's house is in Park Lane. A dour, deeply tanned man in a black suit and a white shirt opens the door and raises his eyebrows. He is wearing an earpiece. Noah, presumably, and obviously Stella never managed to get him on the phone.

'Stella can't make it. I'm taking her place,' I explain shortly.

'We do body searches on people we don't know,' he says, his eyes travelling down my length.

'The fuck you are,' I tell him rudely.

He grins suddenly. 'I like you. You've got balls.'

'Whatever,' I say in a bored voice.

His grin widens. He's got good strong teeth. 'If you've got a weapon hidden in that tight dress you deserve to kill him.'

'It's a uniform,' I say stiffly.

'No kidding,' he leers.

I look at him with raised eyebrows.

'Come with me.'

I step into the mansion, he closes the door, and I follow him into the Mafia Don's residence. What can I say? Wow? Crime really does pay. Yeah, must be nice to have so much. Polished granite, marble columns, fantastic lighting, touches of platinum, sleek black leather trimmings. Nope, not my thing, nevertheless very, very impressive in a cold, masculine sort of way.

He takes me down a curving staircase that appears to go down at least another three floors into the ground. I have heard of such houses. There are more floors underground than above ground. He stops after the second flight of stairs and walking down a corridor, opens the door to what looks like a dimly lit massage room.

He flicks his wrist, looks at his watch, and says. 'He'll be with you in five minutes.'

Then he winks and disappears. I look around the room. Opera music is being piped in through hidden speakers, and it is wonderfully warm. I walk towards the massage table. All the different oils are in a kind of bain-marie on a trolley next to it.

Shit. Suddenly I feel really nervous.

I've never massaged anyone other than Stella and my sister. I take a deep breath. No, I can do this. I will tell my grandchildren about the day I massaged a Russian Mafia boss. I smile to myself. I pick up a bottle of oil. I twist the cap and smell it. Oooo... lavender, musk and something else ... Rosemary?

I pour some on my palm and rub my hands together. The

smell surrounds me. Very nice. I adjust my clothes. I know exactly why the black suit had been staring at me. The uniform is way too tight. I hear a sound outside the door and quickly put my hands to my sides and look towards it.

The door opens and this huge mountain of a man with a small towel slung around his hips comes in. Whoa! I inhale in slow motion. Jesus! No wonder Stella is all tied up in knots. He exudes pure sexual energy. Let me describe him to you. The first thing that hits me after his height and breadth are his incredible tattoos. They cover his body and they are not an untidy collection of random images, but each one subtly connected to the others. For example; an angel smiles at a tiger tearing into an impala, above their heads are intricate images of stars, demons and other strange creatures. On his shoulder a cobra hisses dangerously, its mouth open and hood flared.

The next thing that floors you are his eyes. You know those crazy drawings of Nordic aliens, with their hypnotizing ice-blue eyes? That's what his are like. Piercing and magnetic. Shit. I can't stop staring. Those crazy eyes slide over me, lingering on my breasts, and then pulling back, and narrowing on my face.

I want to smile, but I am frozen.

'Where is …?' He makes a rolling motion with his big, powerful hand. Stella was right; after six months, twice a week, she has not even registered enough for him to even remember her name.

'Stella,' I supply helpfully.

'Where is … Stella?' he asks quietly. His voice is deep and the accent is strong and actually extremely sexy.

I open my mouth to speak, and nothing comes out. I clear my throat. 'She couldn't make it. I'm here to take her place.'

He nods. 'Ok,' and going to the massage table lies on it face down.

I gaze at the splendid body, the muscles gleaming in the dim room, and think of Stella. God, I'm not surprised she's fallen for him. I can feel my blood throbbing in my veins. I want to touch him. My desire is so strong it's as unsettling as a fingernail on a blackboard. It sets my teeth on edge. It's almost like making love. I feel hot and excited. My face feels flushed and I pray he hasn't noticed my hesitation. I take a deep breath. Right. Swedish. Make it hard, Stella is saying in my head.

A light sheen of sweat starts on my body. I wipe my brow with the back of my forearm. I flex my fingers and move forward.

I pick up the oil that has been warming in the hot water. Jesus, suddenly the smell of oil feels too musky and erotic. I gaze at his sinewy neck and feel the hair at the back of my own rise. He is like an animal, a big cat. Sleek and dangerous. I put the musky oil back down and pick up a random bottle.

I pour the warm, lemon scented golden oil on the plateau at the base of his spine. I watch it pool. Then I take a deep breath and open the massage with a long, slow stroke. He doesn't react. I shift my hands down to the two mounds of the gluteal muscles. They are firm, strong and tight ... and bulging insolently.

*Make it hard. He likes it hard.*

I dig down and get to work, careful not to make the mistakes that amateurs make – work too fast. My breathing rate increases, but the man does nothing. Just lies there silently. I move to the front of him, grab his shoulders and push down his back with my thumbs and finger pads.

Smooth and sensuous.

My hands roll back. It is almost hypnotic to feel my palms sliding down the tatted skin, and feel the strong muscles underneath move. By now sweat is running down my back. I am so caught up in the job I do not see his hands move, but they are, without warning, cupping my buttocks. I freeze, more in shock than anything else.

The inert body moved!

I jump back in horror. 'What the hell do you think you're doing?'

He lifts his head and looks at me with those wicked eyes. The light shines directly on his face. Vaguely, I register a white scar that starts at the edge of one eye and runs down the side of his face.

'I figured since you are not a real masseuse you were a hooker.'

'What gave you that crazy impression?' I demand, outraged. How dare he?

His eyes slide down to my breasts. I look down. The scarf is dislodged and my breasts are practically spilling out of my uniform. My ears burn as I pull the scarf upwards and clutch it against my chest.

'Well, I'm *not* a prostitute,' I deny hotly.

His reaction is swift and smooth. He rolls to his side and

lands lightly on his feet like a cat, with grace and lightness unexpected for someone his size. Do Mafia kingpins receive some kind of stealth training? He straightens. His cock is massive and fully erect. Naked and utterly unashamed of his body, he takes a step towards me. Shocked and a little frightened I take a step back, but the wall pulls me up short. He stops a foot away from me, and leaning forward, his palms land on either side of me.

I gaze at him with wide eyes.

'Then why did you massage me like that?' he asks hoarsely.

The breath escapes me in a rush. 'Like what?' I whisper.

'Like you want to taste my cock.'

'I didn't. I don't,' I stutter.

'Then why are you fucking wet?' he asks softly. His eyes drop to my mouth.

'I'm not,' I say clearly.

His hands leave the wall and grab my hips. 'Do you want me to make a liar out of you?' he asks.

'Don't touch me,' I spit.

He pulls me towards his naked body until his rock hard cock twitches against my belly.

A strange languor overtakes me, and I am suddenly struck by the desire to submit. To let him have his way. To let him fuck me hard. Because I know it will be a hard fuck. Yes, I'd be just a nameless fuck, and yes, there will be the walk of shame afterwards, but I can live with all of that. The thing that stops me is the thought of facing Stella.

'How dare you?' I gasp.

He laughs, a humorless, cold laugh. 'Is that a challenge or a fucking invitation?'

'It's a fucking warning,' I say furiously.

Ignoring my fury, he runs his fingers along my inner thigh.

I draw in a sharp breath. 'Let go of me or I'll scream.'

His eyes light up. They are like the underside of certain fish, silvery blue. He lets go of my hips. One of his hands comes up to my face. He drags his thumb along my lower lip while I stare up at him, mesmerized by the naked lust in his eyes. The fingers of his other hand arrive at the apex of my thighs.

'Don't,' I whisper.

He brushes his fingers along the crotch of my panties. There is no expression at all in his face when he finds them soaking wet. Without a word he pushes the material aside and inserts a long finger into me.

Holy fuck. My body starts trembling.

'Don't. I don't want you to,' I order, but even I can hear how weak my voice sounds. My brain is already thinking of his thick girth pounding mercilessly into me.

He withdraws the finger and jams it back in. 'Don't?' he taunts.

Blood rushes to my head and pounds so hard I can't even think.

'I … we … oh … ah … shouldn't.'

He doesn't even bother to answer me. Just keeps up the

steady finger fucking. I am so excited I feel as if I'm already at the point of no return. To my utter shame and humiliation, my body shudders and I climax really hard all over his finger.

He smiles, a condescending, triumphant smile.

Suddenly I feel sick at what I've just allowed him to do to me. Jesus, I've behaved like a cheap slut. I swallow hard. I can't even look him in the eye. How could this have happened to me? He made me come with one finger! And that digit is still inside me and my muscles are contracting helplessly around it.

'Take your finger out of me now,' I say in a cold, hard voice.

'Why? Are you ready for me to replace it with my cock?' he mocks insolently.

I am so inflamed that it seems natural that he should bear the brunt of my fury. My right hand flies up towards his cheek. It never connects. Instead, a band of steel curls around my forearm.

'Don't ever do that again. I don't like it,' he says very softly.

I try to wrench my hand out of his grasp, but it's like someone has poured concrete around it. His impassive eyes watch my puny struggles almost curiously. Like a child watching an insect it has caught before it pulls its wings off.

I take a deep breath. 'Let me go,' I cry.

He curls his finger and starts stroking my inside walls, and I feel my body begin to respond to his manipulation. Oh no. I can't allow him to take total control of my body again. I stare into his eyes.

'Please,' I beg. My voice sounds strange and strangled.

One corner of his mouth lifts. It makes him look at once beautiful and cruel. He pulls his finger out of me and releases my hand. 'Fly away little bird,' he says dismissively.

I feel so ashamed tears start to burn my eyes. No man has ever reduced me to a feeling of such utter lack of worth. To him I am nothing but a sexual object. A thing. He thought I was offering myself, and he just helped himself even after I objected. Now he is just getting rid of me. My knees feel like jelly.

I press my lips together and take a sideways step. Some part of my brain tries to make sense of what has just happened. It's OK, you'll never see him again. No one will ever know what happened here today. It's just one of those inexplicable moments you have never experienced before. A powerful man totally floors an inexperienced idiot!

I straighten my spine. You know what, I can do the walk of shame. So what? I take one step in the direction of the door and another step and then another step. I put my hand on the handle and his voice, like warm honey, pours into my ears.

'Hey, if you ever need help or anything, anything at all, call me.'

I shouldn't have responded. It would have been better, more dignified, to walk out the door without even an acknowledgement that he has spoken. Instead, I whirl around.

'If you think I need more of what you just dished out you are very much mistaken. You can take your arrogant offer and stuff it up your ass.'

'The world is a dangerous place, *rybka*. You don't know when you need a helping hand. It is better to have a friend than an enemy.'

I look at him scornfully. A man like him could never be a friend of mine. He's the exact opposite of me. This man has ice water flowing in his veins. I nearly fainted once at a pearl farm when I found exactly how pearls are harvested. They cut through the flesh of the poor oyster and dig around in its flesh until they locate the pearl. Ugh! He is as unfeeling as those workmen.

'I wouldn't come to you if you were the last fucking man on earth.'

He shrugs. 'One day you will come to me again and you will be eager for what I dish out.'

'You'll die believing that.'

'I made you come harder than you've ever come using just one finger. You'll be back for more,' he says confidently.

I feel heat start climbing up my neck. 'You're a real bastard, aren't you?'

'Like you wouldn't believe.'

I shake my head with disgust. There is no way to win an argument with someone who cannot be made to feel ashamed of their rude and arrogant ways. I open the door and walk out.

## CHAPTER 3 (SAMPLE)

### ZANE

I watch her leave the room and hear the muffled sound of her footsteps go down the best of Italy's pink marble. I hit the button on the intercom. Noah replies almost instantly.

'Get Corrine to come up,' I tell him, and remove my finger from the button.

I open a drawer and take out a condom. I tear it open and fit it onto my dick. The door opens and Corrine slinks in with a seductive smile. She is blonde with long legs and a great pair of tits. She is wearing a semi transparent white blouse, no bra, an extremely short black skirt, and as I have stipulated, no panties.

I don't like wasting time.

I grab her by the wrist and throw her against the wall. She gasps as I rip her top open. Her pink-tipped breasts strain forward. I look at them without any feeling. I am dead inside.

'Suck my nipples, Zane, please,' she begs.

I'm not in the mood for that. If my mouth gets anywhere near those breasts, I'll bite hard enough to leave marks. I feel that vicious.

I hold my hand out and she immediately hooks her leg over it, giving me an uninterrupted view of her shaved, beautifully swollen and creaming sex. I never got to see the other one's pussy. It is her pussy I want to see open and dripping for me. I won't rest until I have her in this position of utter submission. Until the day I train her to hook her leg onto my hand and beg me to suck her nipples and slam hard into her, I won't be satisfied.

I ram my cock directly into Corrine's little hole and she makes a grunting sound. Today the sound irritates me. I place my palm over her mouth and twist her face to the side so that I don't have to look into her eyes, and carry on thrusting hard.

The room fills with the wet sound of my flesh slapping hers. I come in record time, so quickly, in fact, that Corrine moans and desperately rubs her unsatisfied sex against me in a submissive, almost animal like begging gesture. I stay still with my palm covering her mouth and her leg hooked over my hand, until she finds her own release.

Immediately I pull out of her clinging body and turn away, but not before I glimpse into her half-hooded eyes. At the desire and need still shining in them.

'Zane, I—' she whispers.

'Get out,' I say coldly.

I hear the sound of her clothes rustling, a small sulky sniff.

It's nearly time to get rid of her. She leaves and I feel like punching the wall.

'Damn you,' I grate. 'Damn you to hell.'

Get the book at this link:

YOU DON'T OWN ME

# ABOUT THE AUTHOR

Please click on this link to receive news of my latest releases and great giveaways.

http://bit.ly/10e9WdE

and remember

I **LOVE** hearing from readers so by all means come and say hello here:

Printed in Great Britain
by Amazon